A Gold Half Eagle

At the age of twenty-two Hal Chesterton's world is turned on its head. He could never have guessed a blocked watercourse heralded such a disastrous change to his life. His pa's lucky coin, a gold half eagle, responsible for a stroke of good luck, now bears a bitter fruit. For the first time Hal has to stand on his own two feet, and the prospects don't look good. Gunfights, loose women and deception play havoc with his search for the culprit. Hot-headed and vengeful, he is not so easily deterred, but falling for a beautiful young woman clouds his judgment.

A Gold
Half Eagle

Brad Fedden

A Black Horse Western

ROBERT HALE

© Brad Fedden 2017
First published in Great Britain 2017

ISBN 978-0-7198-2491-3

The Crowood Press
The Stable Block
Crowood Lane
Ramsbury
Marlborough
Wiltshire SN8 2HR

www.bhwesterns.com

Robert Hale is an imprint
of The Crowood Press

Typeset by
Derek Doyle & Associates, Shaw Heath
Printed and bound in Great Britain by
CPI Group (UK) Ltd, Croydon, CR0 4YY

CHAPTER 1

The sun was riding high in the Kansas sky and the breeze whipped up little swirls of dust in the yard. Twenty-two-year-old Halford Chesterton mounted his nimble quarter horse ready to ride out to the wind-pump enclosure, where the new cattle were gathered. It was the latest purchase his father had made at the local auction, and included some newly imported Hereford cattle to cross with the local cattle and strengthen the breed. And they needed branding. His father mounted his own horse and the two of them were ready to set off. His ma came out of the ranch house with a packet of bread and cheese, some fruit and a flask of home-brewed beer for the day ahead.

'Now you make sure you're back before sundown,' she warned. 'I don't want no repeat of last night, cold stew ain't no good for anyone.'

His pa was quick to respond. 'Don't you worry none, Mary, we'll be back in good time.'

With that they kicked their horses' flanks and were soon out of the yard and off to the enclosure. Branding is a tedious job, but with the arrangement of wooden railings and gates the two of them managed to usher the cattle through one by one. The air was soon heavy with the acrid smell of burnt hair and hide as Hal's pa applied the branding iron to each beef.

For ten years, since the age of twelve, Hal had been helping his pa on the ranch. Wrestling calves had given him fine muscles, and learning to control a horse with his knees, and one-handed, while roping or shooting, had given him superb horsemanship skills. The shooting had been very hit and miss until his pa showed him how to relax the muscles and stop trying so hard, such that by the age of fifteen he could shoot four out of every five cans off the corral fence from anywhere inside the railing while trotting round the enclosure. One day the ranch would be his and it was in his interest to see that he could take good care of it. He wanted it to prosper, of course, but things are not always what they seem, and Hal couldn't possibly have known that everything was about to come crashing down round him. But for the moment, at least, everything seemed good, as father and son began the arduous work of branding. The sun was hot, the brazier was hot, the cattle were restive and the hours passed slowly.

At last his pa looked up. 'That's the last of the new beeves,' he announced, putting the branding iron aside. The smouldering metal with its design of interlocking Cs for Chas Chesterton was left to cool slowly. He came over to Hal. 'I'm a bit concerned, Hal, about the water level in the cut. I guess we'd better go up-valley to the river and take a look.'

Without adequate water, beeves soon become weak and lose weight. If there is insufficient rainfall or someone interferes with the water supply, quick action has to be taken to remedy the situation. Rainfall was a little low but not yet too little to worry unduly. The pump was pulling up enough. So they were surprised that the stream feeding the enclosure seemed lower than they were expecting. This wasn't the main flow through the ranch but an old cut diverted to water lush calving paddocks.

'Water does look a bit low, Pa.'

'Yeah, log jam or something.'

It took the best part of two hours to meander up-valley to the main river. Beeves were wallowing at one of the watering shallows, but it was soon apparent that there was a blockage of some sort on the distributary stream. As they rode up to the junction of the stream and the river the problem was clear. Brushwood had collected and bunched up making a small blockage, exacerbated by a couple of larger branches off a cottonwood.

'Ain't nothing much,' Hal's pa said. 'Couple of branches, we'll have that cleared in no time. Didn't think it would be much.'

But as Hal got down to pull one of the cottonwood branches free, he suddenly stopped. 'I don't like the look of this. This branch has been cut, it ain't a natural break. Do you suppose. . . ?'

'Just something that's come downriver, that's all.'

But Hal wasn't convinced. 'No Pa, look at this, the brushwood here has been stuck into the mud, it never planted itself like that. An' that's why it's all blocked up.'

His pa looked at the blockage. 'I agree, that ain't natural. But why? I mean we ain't never had anything like this before, why now?'

'Do you reckon I should camp out here a while overnight an' see if anyone shows up?' Hal asked his pa.

His pa stroked his chin. 'Don't reckon that'll do no good. If this was deliberate, it was to draw our attention to somethin'. So best wait and see what next.'

They rode slowly back to the ranch house with little conversation, each deep in his own thoughts. Ma Chesterton had prepared a good hot beef stew laced with potato, carrot and onion and her own blend of oregano and cilantro to give it that distinctive flavour that her husband adored. Conversation was slightly subdued, even after the meal. Hal could see his pa was troubled, but he gave little away in front of his wife. Nothing was said about what they'd seen up the valley.

Hal understood that his pa never wanted to bother his wife with day-to-day worries about the ranch – she had enough to do running the domestic side of things, and over the years they'd fallen into a comfortable separation of duties. They'd always managed on their own without any help except for Hal on the ranch, and hired hands for driving to market every autumn. The ranch had never grown out of hand, just about six hundred head; Hal's pa had concentrated on breeding fine quality into his herd, and his beeves always fetched a good price. But now it seemed someone had got a grudge.

They didn't have to wait long to find out what was going on, for the very next day, two riders came to the ranch. Hal and his pa stood out on the porch to see what they wanted.

'You Mister Chesterton?' said one of the riders.

Hal's pa nodded but said nothing.

'Can we talk inside?' the rider asked.

'We can talk here,' Chas Chesterton replied, his hands stuck firmly into the top of his belt.

'Might be better. . . .'

'Say your piece Mister, and git goin'. I ain't got all day.'

The rider reached into his pocket and unfolded a piece of paper. 'It's about this IOU.'

'IOU?' Chas Chesterton queried. 'What in hell are you talkin' 'bout?'

'I'm talking about ten thousand dollars,' the man replied.

There was a silence while nobody knew what to say. Only one of the riders had spoken so far. Hal was looking at his pa and trying to figure what was going on. His pa was moving his hand slowly towards his gunbelt.

'Don't do that Mister, we ain't got no say over this. We're just messenger boys. An' the message we were told to give you is simple, pay up or there'll be trouble.'

Hal decided to join in. 'You mean like blocking the river?'

'That kind of thing, maybe. Or maybe something else. Point is, if there ain't no payment you won't be in business much longer.'

Ignoring the advice, Hal's pa had moved swiftly and drawn his gun, he fired two quick shots into the dust near the horses' hoofs. 'That's all I got to say. Now skidaddle.'

The horses bucked and the riders at once turned back down the track, quickly reaching a fast trot and disappearing into the distance.

'Was that wise, Pa? I mean they'll only come back or something. What's this about, anyways? Do you owe somebody ten thousand dollars? We ain't never got that kind of dough to spare.'

His pa stepped off the veranda, looked down to the ground and scuffed his boot in the dirt. 'I'd like to tell you, but it's a kinda private matter that I wouldn't want you to know. It was a long time ago.'

'And now someone's calling in the debt. Do you really owe?'

'I did write a note, but it was a kinda joke, it was never goin' to happen.'

'But it has,' Hal said plainly.

'Mebbe,' his pa replied. 'Mebbe.'

'Well, Pa, you mightn't want to tell me about it, but I guess you'd better, just in case anything happens. They weren't joshing, somethin' bad'll happen for sure an' we'd better be ready for it.'

Chas Chesterton looked long and hard at his son. He loved his son beyond anything in the world. The day he was born was the highlight of his life, and he never let it pass without a celebration and a prayer to the Almighty. Of course he loved his wife too, but . . . and here was the but, it now looked as if that happy shivari, a wedding day to remember, was coming back to haunt him in a way he never imagined. How would he ever have thought that the foolish dealing between two young bucks would rear its head in such an ugly manner some twenty and more years later? But it had, and now he must face the consequences. But why now, what had suddenly sparked it off? There was only one thing to be done. He would have to visit his old adversary, his drinking-buddy companion of a misspent youth, and see why he'd decided to call in the IOU.

'I've decided,' he said without embellishment.

'That's good,' Hal rejoined. 'What have you decided?'

'Don't you worry, son. I've got it all figured.'

Hal had never stood up to his pa before, there was no need, but this felt different. He didn't like it. 'Not quite. In a way this ranch belongs to me as much as it belongs to you. I've a right to know what's goin' on. Ten thousand dollars is a big deal and you might be in danger. I don't want nothin' to happen to you, Pa.'

'Well, it's goin' to take a few days to ride out and see my old friend. I guess you could ride along too. Only I don't want to leave Mary on her own, with this matter brewin' up.'

'I'll ride over to our neighbours and see if I can get Ben

to look in an' see everything's all right while we're gone.'

His pa made no objection and Hal felt that his pa was actually glad that he'd offered to accompany him to see his friend. Was he expecting trouble?

Everything was arranged. Ben Holder, the youngest son of their nearest neighbours, said he'd willingly come out to the ranch each day to keep an eye on the calves in the pump enclosure and everything else. Ben was a good rider and handy with a rifle if the need should arise. In any case, Chas Chesterton felt sure nothing would happen before he'd seen his friend to sort out what was going on.

Setting out early the next day, Hal and his pa stopped by in the town to see if anyone had recognized the two riders who'd called out to the ranch. But they drew a blank, it seemed the riders hadn't gone into town at all.

By nightfall on that first day Hal and his pa reached Suttonville, some fifty miles from home. They put their horses into livery and checked into the town's only hotel. At dinner that night Hal plucked up the courage to quiz his pa about the IOU.

'Are you going to tell me, Pa?'

'I suppose I should. You're right, son, and I'm proud of you for keeping on at me, some things have to come out into the open. But before I say anything else, listen up real good. I done a silly thing really 'bout this IOU nonsense. So, let it be a real good lesson for you. Don't never do nothing that you ain't proud of, or that you might one day regret, cos you nivver know when it might come back and bite you in the pants.'

'You regret this thing?'

'Too late for that, and remember whatever happens, I've always . . .'

Hal cut him short. 'Don't go talkin' like that Pa, it don't

feel good.'

They fell silent and concentrated on the steak that had just been set before them. Hal's mind was a whirr of imaginings. What could his pa have done that brought them to this situation? Between mouthfuls, maybe because he found it easier to talk while engaged on another task, Chas Chesterton decided he had to come clean.

'It was over a woman,' he blurted out, to break the silence between them.

Although there was silence between them, the hotel dining room had several guests and Hal wasn't exactly sure what his pa had said.

'A woman?' he repeated incredulously.

'A woman,' his pa repeated unnecessarily. 'A special woman. Mind, she was only a girl at the time. A right purty girl at that, she was a real looker. And she could cook and keep house and I was courting her. We were walking out together. But then one day I found out she'd been walking out with someone else, an' I didn't like that. Well, turns out it was my best buddy, Jim. I was shocked because we were fast friends from childhood. Larks at school and all that. But you see son, there's only one thing comes between a man and his buddies, and that's a woman.'

Hal was slowly eating his steak and listening with all ears. 'So where does the IOU fit into that?'

'I'm coming to it. Be patient.'

'Well, you better eat some of your steak before it gets cold.'

The conversation, or monologue to be exact, came to a halt, as they both made further inroads to the huge slabs of beef on their plates. Then Chas Chesterton clattered his knife and fork on to the tin plate, pushed his chair back from the table and chewed over what to say next.

'Well, me and Jim had to come to some arrangement. It was no use us both courting the same filly. So we made a pact. We both wrote an IOU for ten thousand dollars and put them on a table between us, and whoever lost would get the other man's IOU.'

'Are you telling me . . .'

'Don't interrupt, Hal. This is hard enough as it is. What say we get ourselves some coffee and sit in easy chairs in that there lounge.'

'If you want.'

'Well, sometimes a man's got to be comfortable when he has important things to say.'

They retired to the easy chairs in the hotel's lounge and waited for their coffee to be served.

Chas Chesterton took a gulp of coffee and drummed his fingers on the arm of the chair to muster his thoughts. 'So you see, we took all the coins out of our pockets and chose the best one. I had a lucky gold half eagle which I always carried with me, my pa had given it me on my tenth birthday for reaching double figures. Anyways, I let Jim flip the coin in the air. I called the eagle and it landed up. So I won. That's all there was to it. And that's it.'

'And the IOU?'

'Jim took mine of course, he lost the flip and got my IOU for ten thousand dollars.'

'Just like that? A stupid bet?'

'It was a game, a joke.'

'But not really a joke because you got the girl,' Hal observed, sagely.

'Yes. It was a kinda bet, so he had to back off and I won the girl.'

'On the flip of a coin! I hope she was worth it,' Hal said without thinking.

'It's how you come to be here today,' his pa said, matter of fact.

'Yes, on the trail of an IOU . . .' then Hal paused as the full meaning began to sink in. 'You mean . . .'

'Yes, the girl was Mary.' Chas watched Hal's eyes widen. 'My wife, your mother.'

CHAPTER 2

Early the next morning, after a quick breakfast of thick slices of hickory-smoked bacon and beans, the two men, father and son, walked to the livery with their saddlebags slung over their shoulders. Neither had any inkling of what the day might bring, and there was a fair chance they wouldn't reach their destination before nightfall. So another night in a strange town was in prospect.

'Why would a man do this after all these years?' Chas Chesterton said half to himself and half to anyone who might be listening. 'I mean, it don't seem right.' He turned to his son.

'You know, Hal. I don't like this one little bitty bit. Jim would never have done a thing like this. I can't believe he's changed so much.'

They collected their horses and saddled up as the sun spread its fingers into the nooks and crannies of the livery yard. Hal didn't like the way his pa was talking, but made no reply. He thought his pa might say more, and he was right.

'I know I ain't seen Jim for more 'an twenty year, but I jes' feel if he needed help he'd come right out and ask for it. Last I knew he had his own spread and was doing pretty good.'

Suttonville was just coming to life as they rode down Main Street. Stores were opening their doors, and merchandise was being dragged out on to the boardwalks. The grocer's assistant was stacking sacks of flour and dried beans by the door. At this time of year folk would be running low before the main harvest replenished their stocks and the grocer knew this only too well, a fact reflected in the price displayed on a ticket pinned to the door. They stopped briefly to buy some bread and cheese for the day's journey. There was something comforting about the daily round. Folk busying themselves with their bits of trade and their bartering. The sight of old men occupying their seats on the verandas, where they'd sat for so many years and would still do so for years to come. Matches being struck and smoke curling into the rafters as they chewed over yesterday's news and waited for something to happen today. Carts rumbled along bringing in supplies from the surrounding countryside, while buggies and buckboards were starting to bring shoppers and ladies of leisure into town. A few eyes were cast towards Hal and his pa, strangers in the town, but interest soon passed as they rode out.

Ahead of them stretched a long day of riding. The finger board pointing due north said Crabbie would the next place. Then a turn westwards to find Jim's ranch. The sky was without a cloud and the ride would be arduous, even though the road was well marked and had a passably good surface.

When the sun was at its height around midday they pulled off the track into a culvert and set about brewing some coffee. Hal collected some dry wood while his pa filled their canteen from the river and poured some into a billycan for the coffee. They sat under the shade of tall

16

willows with whispering leaves, drank their coffee and shared the bread and cheese. It was just as they had done many times at home on the ranch. Hal loved riding out with his pa to check on the cattle and make sure the herd was prospering. He'd learned the rudiments of beef husbandry, bits of essential cow doctoring, and just about all there was to know about sweet grass and poisonous herbs. When the time came for him to take over the ranch, he knew he would be good and ready.

The fire was kicked out, tin mugs rinsed out in the river and the horses, refreshed from the break, saddled up. As Hal tightened the cinch, his pa watched him secure the buckle.

'Don't you never let no one do that for you, and always check before you ride off.'

'Pa,' Hal began, in a very resigned voice, 'if you've told me that once, you've told me a hundred times.'

'An' I always will, son, old habits die hard.'

Hal laughed. They mounted up and were soon back on the road. Mile after uneventful mile passed, with the passage of the sun arcing its way across the deep blue Kansan sky. They passed through Crabbie, a two-bit shanty grown beyond its useful size, and took the main track heading west. Hal's pa looked up to the sky and noted the deepening of the colour back east, night was beginning landfall somewhere way out over Virginia or maybe Kentucky already. And it would soon be painting their neck of the woods with long shadows.

'I don't reckon we're going to make any other town by nightfall, should we go back to Crabbie?'

Hal was surprised at his pa's indecision, could there be something else on his mind?

'No point in that, Pa. We might as well sleep under the

stars. Didn't much like the look of that ramshackle saloon as we passed through Crabbie. More 'an likely they'll charge us a high rate being travellers and serve us bad grub.'

His pa nodded agreement and they rode on without further words. At length Hal felt his pa was wrestling with some demon in his brain.

'Pa, what's on your mind? Something's eatin' you up real bad. I ain't never seen you so do-lally.'

'Well, I guess I'm just chewin' over things. I mean I just went right ahead and said let's get on out and see Jim. But I don't really know exactly where his land is or if he's still hereabouts. What if he's moved away somewhere? We could be out on a wild turkey chase.'

This was so unlike his pa that Hal became quite worried about his rambling mutterings. The nearer they seemed to be getting, the more confused his pa was becoming. He tried to bring the conversation back to more practical matters. 'So what was the name of the nearest town where this Jim critter was livin'?'

His pa threw a hand up in the air to dismiss the place. 'It wasn't much of a town, just a few dwellings and a Main Street with a few traders.'

'But that was more'n twenty years ago, Pa, it must have grown since then, and what was it called?'

'Mary Town,' Chas said, with a weary shake of his head.

'Mary Town? That ain't a place name.'

'It sounded like Mary Town. Spelled a little different, but sounded the same. You know when I found out that was where Jim had moved I figured that he still harboured some feelings for the girl who had become my wife. Too much of a coincidence to lose a girl called Mary and then move to Mary Town. I think he regretted the hasty action, tossing a coin. But I never gave him a chance to go back on it. I married your mother three months after I won that toss and we moved right away down south.'

They'd passed a few more miles while that piece of conversation was going on, then Hal spotted a wooden fingerpost. 'Look, Pa, Crabbie back that way, and Marriton 15 miles further on it says.'

'That'd be it!' his pa exclaimed with some relief. 'It still exists, anyways.'

'Well,' Hal noted with an obvious simplicity, 'we ain't goin' to make that by nightfall. We'd best find ourselves a good scrape and settle down for the night.'

His pa didn't need much persuading, and they soon came across a small promontory jutting over a nearly dry watercourse. A miserable stream wound its meandering way down the riverbed. It was a good thing they had already got enough water as this would be too dirty to drink and no good for cooking, either. While his pa hobbled the horses and let them munch the plentiful grass, then unrolled their soogans and kicked out a small patch for their fire, Hal took his rifle and stalked off for some meat. He didn't have to go more than a couple hundred yards to come across a group of rabbits taking their evening meal, and one would be enough for their own dinner. Hal lined his sight on the largest of the group and fired. One shot was all that was needed. The rabbit appeared to leap in the air before falling to the ground, a clean hole through its head.

By the time he got back with the rabbit, his pa had started to build a fire, and by the time the rabbit was skinned and cleaned, the fire had taken hold. His pa pushed the pair of iron cooking rods into the ground and they waited for the fire to calm down. The coffee pot was put on the edge of the heat and once the wood had started turning into glowing charcoal, Hal set the skewered rabbit over the fire. Wild rabbit cooks quickly, there's hardly any fat so none drips off to flare the fire, unlike with slabs of marbled steak which are best cooked in a pan, and they certainly hadn't brought a pan with them, let alone thick juicy steaks. The rabbit meat was enough to satisfy them, eaten with hunks of bread and washed down with strong coffee. They saved the cheese for the morning.

Darkness fell quickly and soon they were sitting beneath a starry sky with an occasional cloud strangely making itself visible by blocking the light from the moon. More wood was chucked on to the fire to give a little more comfort rather than heat. Out on their own ranch under a night sky like this, and with a good fire, they would have been chatting away together, father and son, talking over all the things that fathers and sons talk about. Tonight was not like that. The conversation was disjointed, hesitant, apprehensive.

'Are you worried any, Pa, about seeing Jim after all these years?'

'Haven't given it much thought.'

Hal knew that wasn't true. 'I mean, you're both a lot older, maybe don't even look the same. Did he have a beard? Old men grow beards.'

'We ain't old, son!' his pa corrected pretty damn fast. 'Forty-five ain't old. Ninety's old.'

Hal smiled to himself, and his pa soon smiled too. He clipped Hal's ear playfully. 'You sure are lucky you're too big to go over my knee!'

'Yeah, an' you're lucky you ain't quite small enough yet to go over mine!'

They both roared with laughter.

*

The sun came up bright and early, poking its wheedling fingers into the last vestiges of sleep. The smallest spattering of rain had fallen at some time in the night, just enough to be noticeable like a light dew, but not enough to make anything wet. The horses were already up on their feet, they knew that once there's enough light it's time to eat. Hal was first to emerge from his cocoon, and he quickly gathered a few bits of wood to encourage the embers into enough heat to brew the coffee.

After a meagre breakfast of coffee, cheese and the last chunks of dried bread, they regained the track for Marriton. At the very least they hoped it was a big enough town to supply their food needs for the journey back home.

Needless to say Marriton was now a small township, and when Hal and his pa rode into Main Street, they saw a thriving community going about its business.

'See, Pa, I told you things change.'

'Yeah, I see that. I guess we'd better start making some enquiries, see if any folk here know Jim, and where his ranch is.'

'Does he have a second name?' Hal probed.

'Of course – Jim Crow.'

'Don't be ridiculous, Pa, that ain't his name, and you know it!'

'Well, no. But that's what I used to call him, an' if you'd seen him on the dance floor at the weekly hops you'd know why! His real name was James Crowley. I wouldn't never forget that, would I? Now let's get into this here saloon, The Golden Sunflower, looks friendly enough. We'll have a glass of beer and ask some questions. But first get us some supplies.'

The following hour was not particularly illuminating. They got a few blank stares when they mentioned the name

James Crowley. Folk seemed almost reluctant to acknow-
ledge the name, and only muttered incoherent answers.
Finally Chas could stand the prevarication no longer: he
slammed his glass down on the bar counter and turned to
the startled faces.

'Now listen here, friends, we've come a long trek to find
this here James Crowley, I know he had a ranch in this area,
someone must remember him!'

There was an annoyingly silent response. Chas scanned
the room. His eye caught a man nodding his head. 'You, sir,
you know him?'

'I know him all right,' the man affirmed. 'So do other
folk, but we don't speak of Crowley no more.'

'He's moved away?' Chas asked.

'Kinda. Are you lawmen? Texas Rangers or sumpin'? I
guess they're after him already. Cattle rustlin'. Ranch went
bust and he turned sour. Stole cattle off folk hereabouts,
just a few to start with, then more and more. Folk got angry,
burned him out one night. Nobody ain't seen him since.
His old ranch is a couple miles on up the road, black as the
day it went up, and good riddance.'

'Well, I'm much obliged,' Chas said good naturedly.
'That was as painful as drawing cactus spines out of my foot,
but we got there in the end. Now I'd like to buy ya'll a
drink.' He threw some dollars on the counter and nodded
to Hal to follow him out of the saloon.

'All this was for nothing,' Hal remarked pointedly.

'Not a bit of it,' his pa replied. 'We got all the information we needed. Jim Crowley's been run out of town, mebbe
for rustlin', mebbe on trumped-up charges. I don't make
no judgements until I speak with the accused person
himself.'

'But we're not going to find him here.'

'Mebbe not, and mebbe not at all. But it do look like he might be behind the release of the IOU if he's fallen on bad times. He might need help.'

'How can you say that?' Hal exploded. 'This Crowley spook has sent two riders threatening you with trouble if you don't pay them ten thousand dollars, and you say he might need help, might have fallen on bad times! Geez!'

'Listen, Hal, learn this lesson, boy. Don't judge a man until you know the facts. You are jumping to your own answers, you haven't got one shred of evidence that it was Jim sent those riders. That's how hanging parties conduct their business, and innocent men get their necks stretched. I don't hold with that way of thinking, and neither should you.'

'We might as well go back home, then,' Hal said, rather dejected and smarting from his pa's rebuke, even though it was justified on this occasion. It still hurt being corrected by his pa.

'Not yet, Hal. I want to see Jim's ranch, burnt out or whatever. I need to know something more about the man.'

They mounted up and rode off in the direction of the burnt-out ranch. It wasn't exactly difficult to find, even the wooden ranch gate had been blackened with fire. They rode down the track in silence – it was an eerie place somehow, still full of black deeds as well as charred and blackened timbers. There was still the distinctly acrid smell of a life gone up in flames. It impinged on the nostrils with every step on the ground as if the very place was impregnated with a layer of carbon dust. Truth is, it probably was. The ranch house was no more than a gaunt skeleton, looking like the carcass of a gigantic steer. The outbuildings had been all but razed to the ground. From the size of the buildings' ashen remains, Chas reckoned Jim had had about a thousand head of cattle. That would have been a pretty fine income. Now all gone to dust.

'Listen, son, you're going to find this strange, but we're going to camp here for the night.'

'What? In this ghastly place?'

But Chas said no more, and Hal didn't challenge. His pa had his reasons, and that was that.

In the morning the sun came up on their little camp, nothing more than two soogans and a camp fire. It had seemed almost irreverent the night before gathering up wood and having a fire in a place that had been devastated by flames just a little while previously. Hal didn't question, he felt it wasn't the right thing to do, but his pa did say one thing to him: 'If you want to understand a man, you must live in his house.' Hal thought he understood what his pa meant, but he wasn't sorry to leave that desolate heap of a life gone wrong.

His pa decided there was nothing more to do for now. Searching for Crowley would be a waste of time. They should go back home and wait for Crowley, or whoever, to make their next move. Another night under the stars would be no hardship. In fact, without saying anything, both of them were enjoying the time together and the special bond that man and boy, father and son, can feel when they share the same fire, the same coffee, the same stars. But the worst thing in the world is that good times always come to an end, and the end was about to be as shocking as could possibly be imagined.

CHAPTER 3

The ride home seemed to be taking longer. Half-way they stopped for an overnight camp, but lying in his soogan, the stars had no magic for Hal. His mind was a cauldron of distasteful ideas. He didn't like his pa being in some kind of trouble, he didn't like the thought of there being a ten thousand dollar IOU against his pa, he didn't like the fact that this Jim Crowley seemed to be a bad lot, and the burnt-out ranch had made a horrible impression. All these unpleasant things were giving Hal a hard time. Somehow his pa seemed to remain cheerful. It might have been because he was putting a brave face on things, not wanting to worry Hal, but if so, it didn't work. Hal was worried.

'I can't say I like the turn of events, Pa,' Hal said at last as they sat together drinking their coffee by the morning fire. 'I know you're trying to appear not too concerned, but you can't disguise it. I can tell you're agitated.'

'I don't like it any more'n you do,' his pa admitted. 'Jim was always a fine fellow. This has come as a bit of a shock.'

'Do you think he sent those riders to deliver the IOU?'

'Who else?'

Hal threw the dregs of his coffee into the fire, which hissed its displeasure at being wetted. 'Well, we don't know

25

for sure that Jim had the IOU, suppose someone stole it off him?'

'How would they know who Chas Chesterton was, or how to find me?'

'Yeah, I guess you're right, Pa. C'mon, we need to finish this wild turkey hunt and get back home.'

The fire was even more indignant at being soaked with river water and then scuffed out of existence. They mounted up and regained the road. About a mile from home Hal sneezed.

'That smell of Crowley's burnt buildings kinda hangs around, don't it, Pa? The smell of charred timbers gets right into your nose and lingers. It ain't pleasant.'

'That ain't nothin' to do with Crowley, the wind's blowing up from the south.'

There was a moment of horror as they both looked at each other, and at the same moment realized that the smell was from burnt timber – and it was a lot closer than the lingering smell from out Marriton way. No more words passed between them as they spurred their horses into a gallop. It wasn't long before they knew the worst. Smoke was rising from their land. Dismay soon followed as they realized the fire was all but finished. The ranch, outbuildings, barn and hayloft were not much more than burnt-out shells. It was the same pungent smell, the same choking assault of sharp, dry needles pricking at the nose and throat, the same in every way but one: this was personal – *their* ranch, *their* livelihood, *their* home.

'Dear God,' Hal said, exhaling loudly. 'We need to find Ma.'

'She'll have found safety somewhere in town,' Chas said, unable to disguise the anxiety in his voice. 'I only hope she got out in time. What if . . .'

'That's no way to think, Pa. She'll be safe, nobody would burn a ranch with someone trapped inside.'

'What if she took some shots at them?'

'She might not have seen anything until it was too late, I'd reckon. . . .' But Hal didn't have time to finish his sentence. His pa had dismounted and was hurrying towards the blackened carcass of their ranch house, when he stumbled and fell. Hal jumped straight out of his saddle and rushed to his pa. He scooped him up off the ground and kneeling in the dirt held him in his arms. His pa's eyes were rolling and his mouth had gone slack, he was sweating profusely and breathing in short loud gasps.

'Pa! Pa!' Hal pulled his pa's body closer to his chest and tried to shake him out of his semi-conscious state. 'It's going to be all right, Pa, I've got you safe. Say something to me!'

He put his ear close to his pa's mouth, but all he could hear was the rasping sound of his pa's throat snatching at air. A tear escaped the corner of Hal's eye, he could almost feel his pa slipping away.

For a moment he felt powerless. His eyes were filling. 'No!' he said so quietly to his pa that it was little more than a whisper. 'You can't leave me like this, we've got to find Ma and rebuild. Yes, rebuild, Pa. We'll make it all good again, just like it was, this ain't nothing we can't overcome, but I need you, I need you to help me rebuild . . .' his voice trailed away as choking began to interfere with his voice.

There was no response, but his pa's breathing was slightly less urgent and the snatches went deeper, his eyes had stopped rolling but remained distant, glazed and disconnected. Hal was in a dilemma. He knew he had to get his pa to the doctor, but he couldn't just lift him on to a horse and drape him over a saddle, or even hold him upright and ride into town. He laid his pa carefully on the ground, unrolled his soogan and eased his pa on to it, covering him with the other soogan and placing a saddlebag under his head. His pa had closed his eyes, didn't move at all, but was breathing more normally. He left him there and crossed to the barn, its walls standing black and gaunt, the roof having fallen in. The stored hay must have fuelled a raging blaze. At the far end he could see the partial remains of a buggy, the buckboard and a cart. Only the buggy stood proud of the debris. Hal went to inspect its roadworthiness and was heartened to see that the axle and its two wheels were black but whole, and that although the seat and canopy had disintegrated, it was still serviceable.

Not more than an hour later, Hal had extracted the remains of the buggy from the fallen roof timbers, most of which were still smouldering, and with ingenuity and scavenged pieces of unburnt harness, he was able to rig up a passable form of transport for the difficult task of conveying his pa into town.

It was mid-afternoon when the forlorn equipage arrived in Main Street. It immediately attracted the attention of townsfolk, who came rushing off the boardwalks to help Hal. Amid the bustle of people offering support and assistance Hal pulled up the contraption outside the town's one hotel. Willing hands lifted his pa out of the charred buggy and carried him into the hotel's lounge where he was made comfortable on a sofa. His eyes still seemed a little distant but the signs of life were more encouraging. A small glass of brandy was administered carefully and someone ran off to fetch the doctor. Hal turned to the people gathered round, many of whom he knew well. He was anxious to ask just one question:

'Where's my ma?'

It was greeted with a hesitant murmur and Hal was

immediately aware that things were not good.

It was Mrs Holder, Ben's ma, a close neighbour and friend, who answered: 'The doc's looking after her.'

'But she's OK, Mrs Holder?' Hal hoped.

Mrs Holder looked him in the eye. 'Nope, I can't say that she is, Hal. I wouldn't lie to you. Your ma was in bed when the ranch caught fire, and she barely got out in time.'

'Caught fire?' Hal queried. 'Caught fire? You mean, when it was burnt down. That weren't no ordinary fire from a stove or nothin'. Have you seen the place? It's been burnt to the ground, not just the house, but every darn thing.' Hal's voice was rising in line with the anger that was gaining hold of him.

At this point Sheriff Kelley came into the hotel lounge and said, 'Hal, I'm glad to see you're safe.' Then he saw Hal's pa lying on the sofa. 'Oh boy,' he said, 'this ain't good. What's going on, Hal? Your ma's fightin' fer her life. Your pa looks in a bad way, and your ranch has been burnt out. Too many things goin' on to be an accident.'

'The fire weren't no accident, Sheriff. This is all deliberate, but as yet I don't know why.' He avoided mentioning the IOU or their journey to Marriton and its purpose. There'd be a time to talk about these things, but that time wasn't now. There was a more pressing matter.

'Where's my ma? What do you mean, fighting for her life?'

The sheriff shook his head. 'It's a bad do, Hal. Your ma got caught in the fire. The Holder boy rode into town to raise the alarm, we got people out to the ranch as quickly as possible, but it was too late to do much. Your ma was taken to the doc and he patched her up, but it isn't lookin' good.'

Hal turned to Mrs Holder. 'Where's Ben, did he see what happened?'

The sheriff intervened. 'Ben Holder hasn't been seen since yesterday. Nobody's seen him since he rode back to the ranch. He came into town the speed of light, told me what was happening and rode straight back out. By the time we all got out to the ranch, he was nowhere to be seen.'

There was a flurry at the entrance to the lounge, as people stepped aside to let Doc Steen through to see the patient.

'What have we got here?' he said, putting his bag on the floor and kneeling down beside Chas Chesterton. He looked at his eyes, felt the life vein in his neck, lifted his right arm and put it back at his side. Putting his hand on Chas's brow he turned to Hal. 'Was he sweating?'

'Yeah, he was sweating. I thought he was goin' to die on me. But he's a tough old turkey and I guess he ain't ready to go yet.'

There was a hush in the room while the doc carried on with his brief examination, then said, 'He needs to be in bed and someone to look over him for the next couple of days at least.' He got up, picked up his bag and put a hand on Hal's shoulder. 'You'd better come with me.'

Arrangements were made with the hotel for Chas to be put to bed, and there was no shortage of folk willing to take it in turns to keep watch. Duport was a peaceful town and a good town, and the Chestertons were well liked, and people in small towns like this always rallied round when anyone was in trouble.

Relieved in some ways, but still in a confused state of mind, Hal left the hotel with the sheriff and the doctor.

'You brought your pa in on that?' Sheriff Kelley queried, pointing to the fire-damaged buggy. 'Look, son, I didn't want to say any more in front of those folk. Your ma might not pull through. Prepare yourself for the worst, she ain't a pretty sight, I'm sorry to say. You got any idea what's goin' on?'

'I . . . I don't know,' Hal said, looking down. 'But I sure as hell intend to find out.' He turned to the doctor. 'Doc Steen, tell me my ma's goin' to pull through.'

The doctor just shook his head and took hold of Hal's elbow to walk him across the street to his buggy. 'Hop in, Hal. Eliza's with your ma back at my house.'

It didn't take long to leave the town and turn into the doc's residence. Eliza, his wife, heard the buggy and came to open the door. Hal was deeply troubled by her sad expression, he searched her face for a clue. She looked to her husband and slowly shook her head. Hal jumped down from the buggy and hastened to the door. The doc's wife put out her hand to stop him rushing in.

'Your ma passed away this afternoon, Hal. There weren't nothing to be done to save her. I'm so sorry.'

Hal felt his body go limp as if life was draining from him, too. He stumbled into the arms of the doctor's wife. The doc was on hand to support him, and between the two of them they helped Hal inside and sat him down. The doc poured a glass of something and gave it to him. Hal swallowed it without thinking, his mind was scrambled. He was helped up out the chair and laid lengthways on a sofa. The world turned sideways and began to fade away until nothingness took hold and he descended into a welcome oblivion.

It was some hours later when Hal opened his eyes, the world was still as black as when his eyes were shut. He blinked and stretched. Time had passed and darkness had fallen. The doc had retired to bed, but his wife had placed a quilt over Hal and was still sitting in a chair opposite.

'Hal? Hal, are you awake?' Eliza asked in a gentle voice.

31

Hal heard her strike a match. Lamplight soon spread a warm glow across the room. He eased himself into an upright position. 'Is it night already?'

The doc's wife smiled at him. 'Nearly morning,' she said.

'I'm so sorry, I must have fallen asleep . . .'

She laughed a little. 'Nothing to be sorry about. You needed to shut down while your mind took everything in.'

Hearing that, everything suddenly came back to Hal. He'd come to the doc's house to see his ma, but she was dead; he was in town because his pa was unwell. Gradually he got a grip on his shattered life as the reality of how everything was no longer the same, began to press on his consciousness. He stood up.

'I've got to go and see Pa.'

'All in good time, Hal, there's nothing you can do at this time of day, your pa will be asleep. I'll make us some coffee.' She crossed to the window and held the curtain back. 'Look, it's getting light already. Are you hungry?'

Hal yawned. 'Have you sat up with me all night, Mrs Steen?'

She smiled but made no reply while making her way to the kitchen to put some water in the kettle. She put a frying pan on the stove, poked the embers and put more wood into the firebox. She took a couple of eggs out of a basket. Lifting down one of the sides of pork she cut a thick slice and put it into the pan.

Her husband came into the kitchen. 'Breakfast already? I need some hot water to shave.' He poured some from the kettle and tested it with his finger. 'Just about warm enough. And I'll have some coffee just as soon as it's ready. How's the patient?'

'I'm fine,' Hal said, coming into the kitchen. 'Your wife has been very kind.' There was something else on his mind.

32

'Can I see my ma?'

Doc Steen, his braces hanging loose and his shirt not yet with a collar and stud, said, 'Give me a couple of minutes, Hal.' He took the water and went away to shave.

Eliza turned the bacon in the pan and cracked in the eggs. 'What will you do, Hal? You've nowhere to live. I understand from what your ma managed to say, that everything's been lost.'

'You spoke with my ma?'

'Not really, she was badly burnt, but she did keep whispering "All gone, all gone." It was the only thing she said before losing consciousness.'

No more conversation passed between them. Hal sat at the table, staring into the distance, while the doc's wife attended to the cooking and making the coffee. Doctor Steen came back, clean shaved and dressed. He beckoned to Hal and led him down a passageway to a room at the back of the house. The floor was laid with solid stone slabs like a scullery, and the room was cold. On a wooden trestle lay a body wrapped in a linen winding cloth. It looked too small to be his ma.

'I'll pull back the cloth so you can see this side of her face, but don't try to turn the head.' The doc slowly pulled the cloth back, careful to uncover only one side of Mary's face. The head didn't seem quite right, there wasn't enough hair and the roundness was not complete. The doc could see Hal puzzling.

'It's best not, Hal. The whole of your ma's right side has suffered badly.'

Tears clouded Hal's eyes so he couldn't focus properly. It was probably for the best. He leant down and pressed his lips on to the cold sunken cheek.

'Goodbye, Ma. God bless you.' He turned away quickly

and went back into the kitchen. Eliza put the plate of bacon and eggs in front of Hal and poured him some coffee. The doc sat down next to him. Husband and wife exchanged conversation but Hal heard none of it.

'I'm glad Pa didn't see her like that,' he said out loud.

With breakfast finished, the doctor collected his bag, kissed his wife and put his hand on Hal's shoulder. 'We'll go and take a look at your pa.'

They got into the buggy and rode the short distance into town with few words of conversation. There was little the doctor could say. He knew exactly what the situation would be, and he didn't want to cause Hal any more distress than could be helped.

At the hotel they went to the room where Hal's pa had been put to bed. As they entered, Chas Chesterton's eyes flickered open then closed. Doctor Steen leant over and held back an eyelid. The eye rolled without focusing. There was no movement in the body.

Doc Steen turned to Hal. 'I'm afraid he's not likely to recover properly from this, Hal. Your pa's in a bad way. He won't die, leastways not yet, but he isn't going to walk again, and I don't hold out much hope of him regaining speech. He might, he just might, but it will be very slurred, the muscles down this side of his face have stopped working, just like cutting a hamstring. That doesn't usually repair itself, and there's nothing I can do.'

Hal was silent, and his face had set into a steely fix. His head was held high and his jaw jutted forward. He put his hand on his pa's brow and smoothed the hair off his face. There was another flicker of an eyelid and his eyes opened briefly staring directly at Hal, almost pleading, almost speaking.

'Don't you worry, Pa. You'll get better, I promise. Mrs

34

Holder will look after you while I'm away. I don't know how long I'll be gone, but I'm goin' to find the sonofabitch who's done this to us, and when I do, God help him!'

He turned away and left the room, the doc came hurrying after him. 'Listen Hal, I'll do what I can to see to your pa, you don't need to worry about that, but don't do anything rash and take care of yourself.' The doc stopped in the hotel lobby and watched the angry young man push out through the door.

Hal stepped into the street, the sun rising high in the east – but it held no warmth for him.

CHAPTER 4

Hal left the hotel and walked to the livery where his horse and decrepit cart had been taken. He saddled up, hitched up the cart, and set out for his ranch. Never had such a bright sunny start to the day felt so depressing. He was fired up with anger and hatred, but overlying it all was a deep sorrow for the turn of events, the death of his ma and the poor prospects for his pa making anything like a recovery. Perhaps that would be for the best. Devoted for all these years to his wife Mary, Hal's beloved mother, his pa would surely never recover from the knowledge of what had happened to her.

Thinking these things made Hal even more determined to seek revenge. Was it revenge, or was it justice? Whatever his pa had done could never have justified this turn of events, this horrible outcome. Not for ten thousand, or even ten hundred thousand dollars was death and paralysis a fair consequence. He pulled up in the blackened yard, the raw smell of smoke immediately assailing his nostrils. He unhitched the cart and pushed it into the remains of the barn. The cart was of no further use at the moment, and his horse was glad to be shot of its unfamiliar burden. His next journey was a short one to see the Holders and make temporary arrangements for his pa to be taken care of.

Before he left the yard, he walked over to the ranch house. Little of it was left, but there was debris inside. Not everything gets consumed by fire. Bits and pieces lay around, pots, a broken mirror, a china vase, the stove in the middle of the room. Hal cast his eye over the detritus of a life that had literally gone up in smoke. He wanted to rake through the ashes and find some mementoes, but the sight was too painful. Once again Hal set his jaw and turned his back. This was no longer a place for him.

But then he remembered his pa kept a cash box somewhere in his bedroom. He picked his way back over the smouldering rubble to his parents' room. The bed was a blackened shell of struts. In the corner stood the carcase of the wardrobe which his pa had lovingly crafted in the first year of his marriage. It stood gaunt against the few remaining part-charred pine wallboards. The interior of the wardrobe, once such a fine piece, had fallen in, a mass of charcoal. But under the bits of brittle debris Hal saw the glint of a tin. He poked about with a stick amongst the hot ashes and gingerly lifted out the still warm box.

He hesitated a moment, then prised the lid back. Inside was a wrapped bundle of dollar bills, very warm but undamaged. Hal lifted the package and underneath were a couple of envelopes with old seals. Inside were letters. He didn't stop to read them – they were obviously personal and private, not for his eyes. But then a bright shining coin fell from one of them. There was no mistaking it: it was the gold half eagle. He put it back in the envelope, took the tin, and went back into the yard.

'Well boy,' he said to his horse, taking its muzzle in his hand and stroking its chest, 'it's just you and me, now. You and me, and I ain't really got a clue where to begin. If you think of anything, you just go right on ahead and let me know. You've probably got as much idea as me.'

The horse pulled away and tossed its head. It snorted and stamped a hoof.

'Well, if that's how you feel, we'd better get going.'

In his haste the previous day, Hal had forgotten about his pa's horse, which had wandered off into a paddock. It now put in an appearance trotting into the yard. Hal looked at it. 'You'd better come with me. The Holders will look after you.' He attached his pa's horse to his own saddle, mounted up and rode out.

The Holders' ranch was about a fifteen-minute ride away. Hal pulled up in the yard, scattering some chickens. Mrs Holder came out on to the veranda. She shielded her eyes against the sun to see who it was.

'Hal! I thought it might be Ben.'

'Where's he gone?'

She brushed her floury hands down the side of her apron: it was evidently a baking morning. 'That's just it, we don't know. He rode back out to your ranch after raising the alarm, and has been gone several days now.'

'Well, all our beeves have been taken. I wonder if he was on the trail?'

Just then Mrs Holder spotted a rider coming down the track to the yard. 'That's Ben!' she exclaimed. 'Saints be praised!'

Hal swivelled in his saddle to watch the approaching rider. It was Ben sure enough, but weary and not sitting quite right in the saddle. His left arm was motionless across his lap, a makeshift bandage wrapped round the muscle, and his head wasn't held steady; he was in a daze. Hal jumped out of his saddle, and together with Mrs Holder they lifted Ben off his horse and supported him inside. He was muttering rather incoherently about being shot in the arm, getting one of the bandits in the leg, losing blood himself and riding home without stopping.

Ben's pa and two of his brothers soon came in to see what was going on. Once Ben was properly patched up and had drunk some water and eaten a slab of bacon, he had recovered his senses well enough to speak without slurring his words. He sat up in bed and seemed anxious to talk to Hal. Everyone waited to hear what he had to say.

'. . . so when I got back to the ranch, it was obvious they'd come to raid the beef. Gates were open, the calves were gone from the pump enclosure, and there was no sign of any animals that I could see. When I got out to the furthest end of your land it was easy enough to see where the beeves had been driven. I figured they hadn't got much of a start on me, so I trailed them for a couple o' days and eventually caught up with them. I counted three riders, which didn't seem nowhere near enough to drive your herd, so I waited until nightfall to stampede the herd. I figured they'd never manage to round them all up and so some might be saved from them. Anyways, guns started blasting off in all directions and in the firelight I shot one of them in the leg, but took a bullet myself in the arm. I was just unlucky. I knew I was losing blood, so I bandaged myself as best I could and came on back. I couldn't do any more. So, here I am. I'm sorry, Hal.'

'Nothin' to be sorry about, Ben. You done the best you could and I appreciate that. Don't s'pose you've got any clues about the rustlers?'

'I reckon it would be worth a look at that camp where I stampeded the beef. They must have left something behind. We could ride out there tomorrow and take a look.'

Mrs Holder threw up her hands. 'Ben, you ain't in no fit state to be goin' anywheres.'

'Aww, Ma. I ain't hurt so bad, you seen it yourself, just a flesh wound. I only need one arm to ride.'

Mr Holder calmed his wife. 'The boy's right, best to go lookin' before the trail gets cold. Those beeves are all that Hal's got. I'll ride into town tomorrow and see if there's an appetite for a posse.'

The bedside gathering broke up. Mrs Holder told Hal to stop the night with them and set off the next day; reluctantly she was resigned to Ben riding out, too. Hal discussed what was to be done with his pa, and Mrs Holder readily offered to look after him until Hal got back. She said Mr Holder would take the buggy into town and collect him from the hotel, and Hal wasn't to worry about anything. Mr Holder reassured Hal on that score, and at the same time took Hal's spare horse to the corral. Hal thanked the Holders profusely and said what a blessing it was to have such neighbours. His mind more settled on domestic matters, and with his determination beginning to focus on the rustlers, Hal slept more easy that night.

At sunrise, he was wakened by Ben quietly opening the door. He stumbled into the room and bumped into the bed. Hal laughed.

'Time we were moving out,' Ben said in a half whisper, not wanting to disturb the household. 'I've put some bacon in a pan and the water's just about ready for coffee.'

This much was music to Hal's ears – there was nothing he liked better than an early start with bacon and coffee.

The two of them were soon mounting up in the yard, thinking they hadn't woken anybody else, but just as they were about to depart, the ranch door opened and Mrs Holder came out on to the veranda, a dressing gown wrapped tightly round her.

'Ben, promise me you'll come straight back home when you've shown Hal where that camp was. You're not to go riding off for days on end. It might be only a flesh wound, but . . .'

Ben shook his head at his ma's concern and laughed. 'I promise, Ma. There ain't no point in me going off with Hal. I can't shoot with one hand and hold the horse with it as well, an' if I can't shoot I ain't going to be no use to Hal.'

Then in a mischievous act of horsemanship Ben turned his horse using only his knees while taking his hat off with his one useful hand and waving it in the air as the two of them trotted off up the track.

'Don't you tease me, Ben Holder!' his ma shouted after him, waving her fist in mock anger. She pulled the dressing gown even tighter around her shivering frame, and went back inside, muttering to herself.

Two days riding brought Hal and Ben to a low bluff overlooking a ravine where Ben indicated the remains of a rough overnight camp. The fire, long since cold, had been left to burn out, a sure sign the campers had left in a hurry.

'This is where I came across them,' Ben said, nursing his arm as if the memory were causing fresh pain. 'Not much left to see here, we exchanged a few shots before I took a hit in the arm and decided to make good my escape, but not before I had stampeded the beef. I figured that if the beeves were scattered it would take them a fair while to round them up, and there was always the chance that some might get away and be left behind. The brand would be easy enough to trace back to your ranch.'

Hal had dismounted; he was deep in thought, poking around absent-mindedly with his boot. 'You know, by my reckoning we can't be that far from a small town called Marriton,' Hal surmised. 'That raises an interesting question.'

'Oh? What's that?'

'Well, it can't be a coincidence that I came out this way with my pa to try and trace a man who might have been behind the IOU.'

'IOU?' Ben queried.

'Don't worry about that bit, but we were searching for a man by the name of James Crowley, a suspected cattle rustler, and he had a ranch near Marriton. Leastways, he once had a ranch, so we were told, but when we took a look it was burnt down and he'd been run out of town. If we're going to find out anything else, we'd better head off to Marriton, it can't be far.'

Regaining the main roadway and using the passage of the sun and shadows for direction, the two young men eventually came across a fingerboard which indicated Marriton a further five miles to the west. The shadows were lengthening when they rode into Main Street.

'We'll avoid that saloon,' Hal said pointing to The Golden Sunflower. 'We got a hostile reception there and I don't want folk remembering me.'

They rode on down the street, still busy towards the end of the day with carts and buckboards coming and going, and pulled up outside 'Sal's Saloon'. They checked in for an overnight stay, rode their horses to livery and strolled back through the town.

Suddenly there was a tremendous commotion as people scattered from the street, running every whichway. Shots rang out as four riders galloped into town kicking up clouds of dust and pulling up outside the sheriff's office. Hal and Ben instinctively took cover on the boardwalk and watched two of the riders burst in through the office door. A single shot was fired. The other two riders were stationed back to back in the street, guns drawn, and watching both directions for any sign of hostility. Hal noticed there were five horses: they'd clearly come to spring a friend.

'That can't be good news,' Hal whispered to Ben. 'Whatever they're doin' ain't right.' His hand moved slowly to his six-gun, his fingers twitching in indecision, whether to draw and what to do. 'We can't just stand by and watch.'

'Not our fight. Not much we can do,' Ben replied, crouching lower behind the rail, hoping the action would soon come to a conclusion.

They both looked up and down the street to see if any of the townsfolk looked like they might stand up to the four gunmen, but all they could see were people taking cover behind whatever might afford some protection.

At that moment, the two riders and another man came out from the sheriff's office, looking carefully up and down the street before approaching their horses. Then all hell broke loose, as half-a-dozen armed men spilled out of The Golden Sunflower. Gunshots rang all round the place and bullets whizzed left and right, splintering woodwork and breaking glass. Some townsfolk clearly didn't like the idea of their sheriff's office being raided. Hal needed no further spur to action and drawing his revolver fired off four quick shots towards the raiders. The burst of fire from all the guns brought down two of the five men, one was clearly shot to death, falling limply to the ground, and another, half mounted, took a bullet in the leg and was dragged down the street before falling free and crashing into the boardwalk. The three other riders, seeing the lie of the land, made good their escape.

Hal and Ben rushed out with the other armed men and

quickly surrounded the fallen rider. He was badly injured, leg broken in a nasty fracture with a bleeding wound. He was carried away to the sheriff's office, where, screaming in agony he was laid on a pallet in a cell to await medical attention. The sheriff, nursing a bleeding hand, came out into the street and started thanking his fellow townsmen who'd come out shooting and foiled the raid.

'Not such a peaceful town,' Hal said to Ben. 'We'd best lie low tonight, and ask some questions tomorrow.' They started walking toward Sal's Saloon. But their progress was interrupted.

One of the gunmen, wearing a deputy's badge, came up to Hal. The cylinder of his shooter was open and he was reloading from his gunbelt. 'What's your name, sonny?'

'We're just passing through, staying at Sal's Saloon for the night,' Hal said quickly.

'Name?' the deputy repeated.

'Hal, Hal Chesterton.'

'And what's your business in Marriton, sonny?'

Hal didn't like the repeated use of sonny, it was patronising, but the man was wearing a deputy's badge and Hal was careful to stay calm. He decided to answer truthfully. 'Me and my friend here are on the trail of some cattle rustlers. Stole all the beef off our ranch. They passed near here a few days ago.'

'What's your evidence for that? Convenient you turn up during a raid. You sure you're not part of this band of outlaws?'

Hal handed the deputy his gun. 'Look, you can see I fired off four shots at the raiders, I couldn't exactly be one of them and do that.'

'Maybe not,' admitted the deputy, handing Hal's gun back to him. 'Come into the sheriff's office tomorrow morning. I might want to talk to you. And don't go leaving town before that or I might come looking for you, Hal Chesterton.'

'I won't,' Hal replied respectfully.

The deputy walked away and engaged in conversation with the sheriff. Hal couldn't hear what they were saying, but the sheriff took a long hard look in their direction. They made their way back to Sal's Saloon.

'I don't know what to make of that,' Hal said to Ben. 'He seemed friendly enough, but what if they aren't convinced about our story?'

'Should we leave tonight?'

'Too risky, he's got my name and I think he was serious about coming after us.'

They pushed through the batwings into Sal's and ordered a substantial meal. Apprehensively they spent an hour over some glasses of beer trying to make sure their story was plausible before turning in for the night. The last thing they needed were complications with law officers who couldn't always be trusted. After all, on the face of it, they were two young men who turned up at the same time as a jail break was attempted. Ben was carrying an injury from a gunfight, while Hal had loosed off four shots at someone. The sheriff might still conclude they were part of the gang.

All these things were whirring round in Hal's head as he tossed from side to side, unable to settle on the lumpy pillow. By the time morning arrived he hardly felt rested, and was actually more agitated, anticipating the possible outcomes of visiting the sheriff's office and mistakenly being linked to the three escaped riders.

CHAPTER 5

The following morning after a hearty breakfast Hal and Ben cleared up their things and went off to the livery stable to check on their mounts. They loaded up their saddlebags and walked their horses down Main Street to the sheriff's office. They hitched them to the rail and with a certain amount of trepidation opened the door.

'What if they detain us?' Ben whispered.

'They won't.' Hal reassured him, but he didn't sound very convincing.

The sheriff was sitting behind his desk cleaning a Winchester, the deputy was taking a cup of coffee through to the cells. As soon as they were both inside the door, the sheriff looked up. Nervously, Hal spoke without thinking.

'Did he make it through the night?' he asked.

'Who?' said the sheriff.

Hal pointed to the cells where the deputy was unlocking the door. 'The injured man.'

'And what's that to you?'

Hal shifted his stance uneasily. 'Nothing, just making conversation.'

'I don't need no casual conversation at this time of day,' the sheriff pointed out gruffly, rolling himself a smoke. 'I want to know what the hell you two are doing in Marriton at the same time as a jail break. I've had a look through our wanted files and I can't see no description that matches you, Hal Chesterton. What's your partner's name?'

Ben stepped forward. 'Ben Holder, Sheriff. I tracked some cattle rustlers from down south at Duport . . .'

'Yeah, I know Duport,' the sheriff acknowledged. 'Go on.'

'Well, they were rustled off Hal's ranch, Hal's pa's ranch, the Crossed Cs. I tracked them to an overnight camp a few miles to the south west of here, and there was a shoot-out as I stampeded the beeves to make it more difficult for the rustlers, hoping that some of the beef might not be found by the rustlers but by somebody else who might be honest enough to trace the brand back to the Chestertons.'

The sheriff put down the Winchester, pushed his chair back and put his spurred boots on his desk. His eyes narrowed as he blew out a cloud of fragrant smoke. 'Is that how you got that injury?'

'Yes, sir. It's only a flesh wound. . . .'

The sheriff was quick to interrupt. 'Which you could have done yourself. And now you're both back to try and find the cattle and join up with the rustlers. Are you stealing off your own pa, Hal Chesterton? Sounds like it to me. And pretty elaborate at that. I guess you know this man we've got in the cell.'

'I certainly do not,' Hal asserted vehemently.

'Perhaps you'd better take a closer look.'

The sheriff stood up rather suddenly. 'Let's see if he knows you.' He indicated for Hal and Ben to walk through to the cells. The deputy was standing by the pallet bed, the injured man was propped up on his elbow, the coffee mug in his free hand. Hal took one look at the man's face and was horrified.

The sheriff spoke to the prisoner, pushing Hal forward into the cell. 'Do you know this man? His name's Hal Chesterton.'

The prisoner spat and looked away. 'Never seen him before.'

The sheriff turned to Hal with a look of dissatisfaction. 'That's what I expected him to say. But I was looking at your face, Mr Chesterton, and that told a different story, didn't it?'

Hal threw his hands up in resignation. 'I can explain it. Yes, I've seen this man before, and he knows it.'

'He says he doesn't.'

Hal was insistent. 'Well, he's lying. He's certainly seen me before. He came to our ranch before all this trouble began.'

'Ah,' said the sheriff, triumphantly. 'Now we're getting somewhere. He came to arrange for the rustling of your pa's herd, did he? You're in this together, I guess.' He turned to his deputy. 'Jesson, open the other cell and put these two in to chew over their story while we make some more enquiries.'

'But . . .' Hal began, then thought better of it as Deputy Jesson unlocked the cell door and indicated for them to go in. Meekly they resigned themselves to a period of quiet reflection, confident that the truth would not be hidden for long. When they were sitting rather forlornly on their own, Hal turned to Ben.

He whispered, 'You know, Ben, there's one good thing going on here. That injured man is one of the riders that turned up at our ranch to warn my pa about the IOU. That's why I recognized him. I need to make him think we've come to identify the rustlers, and if we do, he knows he'll hang for it. This'll turn round, you'll see.'

'Maybe,' Ben said, with an undisguised overtone of misgiving.

It was an hour later, maybe two – Hal found it hard to gauge the passage of time sitting in the cell – there was further commotion as riders could be heard pulling up outside the sheriff's office. The sheriff took his feet off the desk, took up his revolver and started to get up. Jesson drew his six-gun and looked out through the window.

'Four riders,' Jesson reported to the sheriff.

'Always in fours,' the sheriff muttered.

The office door swung open. Hal and Ben's eyes lit up as they saw a familiar figure stride into the room, spurs jingling, and three heavily armed men standing behind.

'I believe you've got my son in here,' said the man, approaching the sheriff's desk. Then turning towards the cells. 'That's him in there. Now, tell me what in hell is going on.'

In his accustomed manner, the sheriff's eyes narrowed to help him sum up the situation. Deputy Jesson remained calm but kept his gun at hip level.

'Don't do nothin' hasty,' the sheriff warned. 'I'm Sheriff Chuck Skeeter. You must be Mr Chesterton if that's your boy. Well, maybe we'll get this sorted out sooner than I expected.'

'You're darn right we will,' came the reply. 'But my name's Chuck Holder, not Chesterton, and that's my son Ben. And that's our neighbour's boy Hal Chesterton. His pa is incapacitated. On what charge are you holding them?'

The sheriff gestured vaguely with his hands, indicating that nothing had quite been decided. 'Cattle rustling seems to be . . .'

He didn't get time to finish his sentence. 'Idiot! It's Hal's cattle have been rustled, and these three men have come up with me from Duport to pick up the trail.'

'Yeah,' drawled the sheriff. 'I know it's his cattle but there's a suggestion that he might have been involved in it.'

'What!' exclaimed Chuck. 'You ain't fit to wear that badge if you can't recognize two honest boys when you see 'em. That boy has lost his ma in a fire. His pa's in a bad way. He's suffered enough these last days, he don't need this.'

The sheriff softened. He indicated the various sticks of furniture in the room. 'Let's all stay calm. Sit down, Mr Holder. You riders as well. Give me the whole story an' we'll see where we go from there.'

Hal and Ben were brought out of the cell to join in the explanations which, being washed down with mugs of coffee, took the best part of the next hour. At the end of the accounts, the sheriff was satisfied that the truth had been told.

'Well, now,' the sheriff said, 'It seems that this here man in the other cell is part of that rustlin' gang. We'll hang him for that, and he's got a nasty injury which might turn gangrenous and do for him in any case. Do you want to question him and see what he knows?'

'I sure do,' Hal asserted, jumping at the opportunity. He got up and walked to the cell.

The sheriff instructed Deputy Jesson to let Hal into the cell and stay with him while he got whatever information he could. They all clustered nearby so they could hear what was being said.

Hal jumped directly into the questioning. 'You've seen me before, haven't you? You came to the ranch about the IOU. Were you part of that raiding party that stole our herd and set fire to the ranch? Were you?'

The man shrugged, which annoyed Hal, who raised a fist

ready to land a blow, but Jesson was quick to hold him back.

'That ain't no way to question him,' Jesson said. 'The sheriff's given you an opportunity, don't waste it.'

'All right,' Hal replied calming down. 'Listen mister, you're done for, one way or another. Your buddies ain't coming back. You can do a bit of good by giving me a name or two because I'm going to trail those bastards until every last one of them is brought to justice.'

The sheriff came forward and interrupted at this point. 'Listen, son,' he said to the injured man, 'I can put in a good word for you if you co-operate and maybe you'll get jail instead of a neck-stretch. Just tell me you weren't part of the raid, and give this young man the names of those who were.'

There was a silent pause as everyone waited to see what the answer would be.

The man turned himself over to face the gathering. With a grimace he propped himself up on one elbow. 'All right. I'll talk.'

Eager to get the information he was after, Hal jumped in again. 'Do you know a man named Jim Crowley?'

'Jim Crowley? No, I ain't never heard that name.'

'Let the man tell you what he knows,' the sheriff said impatiently to Hal, then turning to the prisoner, 'Go on, spill the beans.'

'All I know is that it was somethin' to do with a heap of money, thousands I was told, and some of it would be mine in due course. If the man didn't pay up we were to take the cattle. Well, when we went to the ranch there wasn't no man there, just this old woman . . .'

Hal pushed forward and whacked the man round the mouth. 'That was my ma!'

Jesson stepped in again and pulled Hal back. The prisoner wiped a trickle of blood from the side of his mouth.

'I had nothin' to do with the fire. I don't know how that happened. The woman got a shotgun and loosed off a couple of shots at us. I think that was when things turned nasty.'

'Names.' Hal insisted. 'Give me the names!'

'Look mister, I'm dead anyway. I don't need to give you no names. I ain't goin' to give . . .'

This time it was Jesson who came forward and gently put his hand on the man's bandaged leg. Then he pressed a little harder and the man let out a deafening scream of agony.

'I can break the other one too, if you like,' Jesson warned him. 'Now give him the names or this fracture might just break out and you might bleed to death before we can get the doc . . .'

'All right,' the prisoner gasped. 'All right. Corey, Davey, Brent and Norell.'

Jesson lightly pressed the injury again. 'And which is the one we've shot?'

'Corey.'

'Who's the leader? And what's the plan?' Hal demanded.

'Bart Norell's the leader. We've got to sell the cattle and take the money to Mr C in St Louis. More 'an that I dunno.'

This time Jesson pressed the injured leg so hard the man screamed out loud before passing into unconsciousness.

The gathering returned to the sheriff's desk. He sat down. 'Now, you've got what you need to know,' he began, 'What are you going to do next?'

It was Mr Holder who took up the conversation. 'First off, we'll be going after the herd. I want those beeves back where they belong before they alter the brands.'

'All right,' said the sheriff. 'I'll agree to that, and take

these two young men with you so they're out of my jurisdiction.'

Shortly after midday, all six of the men from Duport
mounted up and rode out of Marriton. Ben's pa had taken
the lead. 'The herd can't be that far away if they left it yesterday to ride back into Marriton to try and rescue the
prisoner. I reckon we can track them down, couple days at
most.'

Everyone was in agreement. There were six of them and
only three rustlers, the outcome was assured once they
caught up with the herd. By the time they set up camp that
evening they knew they were on the beeves' tracks, and by
the end of the next day, the dung heaps were soft and
warm, so it was evident the herd was close. Instead of stopping to set up camp the second night, the six-man posse
decided to press on slowly and take the rustlers down
during the night.

They followed the trail by the pale light of the moon.
Passing clouds covered the moon and spread a black
blanket across the land, temporarily plunging the party into
semi-darkness, but after three hours of slow and careful
riding there came the unmistakable smell of cattle at rest,
and the driftings of smoke from a camp fire. Hal wondered
how many of the herd had wandered off during the drive
and got lost, especially after Ben had scattered them a few
nights ago. Hopefully most of the herd was still intact. The
IOU had been for ten thousand dollars and there was a lot
more value than that in the beef now just a stone's throw
ahead of them.

The difficulty was to surprise the camp without stampeding the cattle. The rustlers numbered just three, but
stampeding cattle could throw the whole game into the air
and cause huge problems for the posse. Stealth would be

the best option. Chuck Holder was just outlining plans to dispatch all three rustlers silently with knives. But the gods had other plans for them, and there was an unexpected flash of lightning, followed almost immediately by a tremendous crashing of thunder. The heavens opened, and within moments everyone was drenched. The camp was suddenly alive as horses snorted and cattle stirred. On the spur of the moment Hal took the initiative and drawing his revolver, burst into the midst of the camp shooting at the human outlines. It was almost impossible to see what was happening and consequently Chuck held back the rest of party in case anyone shot Hal by mistake.

Then the sudden storm moved away as fast as it had descended and a scene of some devastation could just be discerned by the returning light of the moon. Another flash of lightning struck away to the west and the gap before the thunder clearly indicated it had already moved many miles away. Yet it couldn't have been timed worse for the posse. The beeves had scattered, there was one corpse on the ground, and no sign of anyone else. Chuck wanted to upbraid Hal for his rash action, but thought better of it, there was nothing to be gained through recriminations.

'Dang it,' Chuck said, 'that's torn a big hole in everything. I guess that one's dead and the other two have made off. We need to get round the cattle before they disappear into the night.'

Without further ado, all six riders spread out to circle the beef. It being dark the cattle were unsure what to do, and after the first scattering most of the herd milled around lowing and snorting; they were not inclined to rush headlong into the darkness. It was the one good thing in an otherwise bad lot. Hal was kicking himself for being so impetuous, but when they were all back together with the beef encircled, Chuck Holder gave him some comfort by saying that it was probably the best outcome they could expect – most of the beef saved, another rustler down, and the other two escaped, but empty-handed.

The rainstorm had left the ground sodden. Nobody was going to lay down any bedroll on that. Two were assigned to first watch, while the others unsaddled their mounts, removed their slickers, made the horses lie down and then propped themselves against the animals lying on blankets on top of their slickers. There wasn't much of the night left, but thankfully it passed peacefully until dawn.

First light brought everyone to their senses, and coffee and bacon were soon on the go using the reinvigorated embers of the rustlers' fire, which the rain had failed to quench. Breakfast brought a welcome rise in spirits, and conversation was soon well under way. A quick count of the beef had given Hal a pleasant surprise, as there were still over five hundred head together, and no doubt some of the others would eventually be returned by honest folk as they discovered the brands.

Hal had made up his mind what was to happen next.

'I want to thank you all for your help. Ben, we wouldn't even be here if it hadn't been for you giving chase on that first day. And Mr Holder, I guess me and Ben might still be in jail if you hadn't come along. But now I want to go on alone. I've got some tracking to do and I intend to do it until I catch up with those last two sonsofbitches and find out who's been behind this.'

'But you'll need help,' Ben said.

'I've had all the help I need, thanks,' Hal replied, not ungraciously. 'This is now between me and whoever I find at the end of the trail. The only thing I need now is for you folk to drive the beef back to my burnt-out ranch, and Ben, can you take care of things until I get back?'

Chuck Holder reassured him. 'We'll do that for sure, Hal, don't you worry. Just take care and remember your pa will want to see you back safe.'

There was nothing more to be said. Hal saddled up and took his leave, thanking everyone again and feeling just the slightest hint of trepidation at the thought of the task before him. But his mind was made up. St Louis was the name of the place he'd been given, so he lightly pushed his spurs into the horse's flank, and without a backward glance, set off for St Louis without knowing either where or how far that might be.

CHAPTER 6

Hal was used to riding on his own. He'd spent many hours riding round the ranch checking on the beef, clearing out watercourses, hunting wolves and coyotes. But he'd usually finished the day back at the ranch, sitting down to a hearty meal which his ma had prepared. He swallowed hard at the memory, and brushed his sleeve across the dampness in his eyes. The sun was directly in his gaze, causing his eyes to water. But then he knew it wasn't really the sun. His ma was dead and buried, his pa was crippled and would probably never walk again, maybe never be able to speak properly. The world was turned upside down, and Hal couldn't stop the tears gathering pace.

His pa would have upbraided him immediately. Hal remembered how his pa had chided him once when Hal had hurt his hand with a hammer blow. *Go and bake a pie, I only need boys to help with men's work, not girls.* Hal had pushed his little chin forward and wiped away the tears with the back of his hand saying, *No tears pa, I'm a boy again, I don't do no baking.* He was probably only three or four at the time. But now he couldn't stop those same tears, the ones he'd always forced back. He choked involuntarily, and throwing his head back, let out a roaring scream of anguish. The tears ran for his ma, then stopped almost at once as he regained composure. He knew they would never come again.

The immediate problem was his headstrong nature, which had made him spur his horse into action without really knowing which way to go. The injured man in Marriton jail had simply mentioned St Louis, and Hal had a vague idea that St Louis was a large town on the Missouri river. They were both just names, St Louis, Missouri, nothing more. His pa had said the rivers on their land all ended up in the east flowing into the mighty Missouri. If the river was mighty perhaps St Louis was mighty, too. Anyway, Hal knew all the rivers in their region flowed ultimately to the east, so it was towards the east that he went.

The first day was tedious, but it gave Hal a chance to reflect on what he was doing and why. He knew he would never be able to look his pa in the eye until he had brought this whole shebang of ideas to a satisfactory conclusion. Three of the rustlers were now accounted for. His pa would be proud of him having shot one of them himself. Thinking of his pa strengthened his resolve, and when he pitched camp that night he looked up at the sky mindful of the Kansas motto that his pa had repeated often enough: *ad astra per aspera* – to the stars through hardship and difficulty. The journey was just beginning, and he slept with an easy conscience.

The second day was a tougher ride as rain swept across the open grassland right into mid-morning. Eventually the sun dried him out, and by early evening he arrived in the small township of Cutler's Creek. Putting his horse into livery Hal walked across the street to the only saloon, which unimaginatively went by the name of Cutler's Saloon. He opened the door and walked in. It was strangely subdued, a few regulars standing at the counter, an old-timer dozing in a stickback chair by the door, and a couple of rough-looking slouchers sat at a table. Hal ordered a beer from the barkeep and asked about a room for the night. The barkeep, in a somewhat surly manner, put down his cloth and the glass that he was wiping, went through to a back room and returned shortly. He said nothing.

A woman appeared from the back room and approached Hal. She had just sprayed herself with a rather strong perfume which assailed Hal's nostrils. Her lipstick was too red and too thick. She smiled at Hal in a knowing kind of way and led him through a curtain to a stairwell. She opened a register on the little wooden table at the foot of the stairs.

'You want a room for the night?' she said, pushing herself forward in an over-familiar gesture. 'That'll be four dollars with breakfast. You do want breakfast don't you?' she said, with an undue emphasis, and smiling all the while.

'I do.'

He signed the register while she watched him write.

'Hal. That's a fine name,' she said.

'Perhaps I could see the room?' Hal said, for no good reason but feeling he needed to make some sort of conversation to avert the woman's unsettling gaze.

'Of course. Follow me.'

Her posterior wiggled up the stairs in front of Hal's eyes. She took too long to make the ascent and Hal had a strong sense of foreboding. This was unfamiliar territory for him. She led him down a short corridor and opened a door at the end.

'This do?' she asked, leaning back against the door so he had to brush past her to get into the room.

He glanced round at the bits of furniture. A wardrobe, a table with washbowl and jug, a bed and a night table with an oil lamp. He pressed the mattress on the bed.

'It's nice and soft,' she said.

'Thank you ma'am, the room's fine.'

'The name's Angie,' she said. 'Not ma'am, makes me sound so old.' She shrugged and giggled. Hal was not impressed. She could be twice his age and looked a little tired at the corners. There was the vestige of prettiness in her face, she had good features, fine bones, but the blonde hair was losing its lustre and if Hal had been more worldly wise he would have noticed that the discoloured whites of her eyes suggested a dependency on drink.

'Are you just passing through?'

'Yes ma'am.'

'Angie.'

Hal hesitated. 'Yes, Angie. Just passing through.'

'And where are you headed?'

'St Louis.'

'That's a long way to be going on your own. You got business in St Louis? Yes, I bet you have, a big strong boy like you, all sorts of business. What sort of business exactly, Hal?'

Probably through fatigue and a little bit of unfamiliarity in the company of a lone woman, Hal blurted out what he hadn't intended to say. 'I'm on the trail of two cattle thieves.'

'A bounty hunter!' Angie's eyes lit up like a gas mantle. She reached out and stroked his arm. 'With muscles like that I bet you could wring their necks soon as look at them.'

'No, ma'am, it's not like that.'

She walked over to the bed and sat on the edge. 'You're wondering if they came this way. Perhaps they stayed here. Come and sit down and tell me what they look like.' She patted the bed and smiled at Hal. He paused, then sat down beside her, but was careful to make sure the distance allowed no close contact.

Angie moved closer. 'So what were they like?'

'I can't say exactly, I haven't seen them close up.' Then

60

he thought for a moment, maybe he had seen one of them, the other one that came to the ranch. Could he remember his features? He tried but failed. What came back to him about that incident was his pa firing off two shots to warn the riders off and send them packing.

'I ain't no bounty hunter, ma'am. The beeves they stole belong to me and my pa. We nearly caught them north of Marriton. We got the beeves but the rustlers got away, at least two of them did. I shot one of them.'

Angie looked at him with admiration. 'You know how to handle a gun, then.'

'They killed my ma. Burnt our ranch down while me and my pa were riding north looking for information. My pa took it bad and I don't know if he'll rightly recover. I won't rest until I find out who was behind it. It weren't just a raid on our beef, there was more to it than that. Now I got three names to go on. Davey, Brent and Norell, don't know which one of them I shot.'

'Davey.'

'What?' Hal turned to Angie in surprise.

'You shot Davey.'

'How would you know that?'

'I don't know for sure. I'm guessin'. Happens we had two strangers stayed here the other night. Names in the register are Nickel Brent and Bart Norell. We don't get so many stopping by that I wouldn't remember names.'

'They stayed here?'

'Yes, Hal, they did, and I might be able to give you a proper description.'

Was this just a lucky coincidence? Hal wasted no time in pumping what information he could get from the woman sitting too close on the bed next to him. He was now sure it was Brent who had come to the ranch to demand the

61

repayment of the IOU. He'd said they were just messenger boys, so maybe Norell was the leader.

'Was one of them taking the lead in things?'

Angie nodded. 'Norell was giving all the orders, he paid for the room, the food and everything, the other one was just his side-kick.'

'Did you hear them say anything about where they were going?'

Angie gave an enigmatic smile. 'Bart told me quite a bit about what he was doing. He just couldn't stop talking about everything, in between . . .'

'In between?'

'You know, Hal, in between things, when he wasn't concentrating on . . . on you know.'

'No, ma'am, I guess I don't know what you mean.'

'Never mind,' Angie said getting up and smoothing the bed cover. 'You'll see what I mean.' She smiled at him and walked to the door, then turned round and winked. 'Now, you'll be wanting some dinner to keep your strength up, won't you? I've got a mighty fine beef pie in the oven. You like beef pie?'

'I sure do, ma'am.'

'Good,' she said. 'So do I!' Leaving Hal wondering what she meant.

Hal had no complaints about the food. Angie served him herself, cutting a large square of pie and scooping out succulent chunks of soft beef and a rich vegetable gravy. Potatoes and carrots were heaped on to his plate and she gave him another enigmatic smile. Her husband came over from the bar with a glass of beer.

'Mind how you go, son. Stronger men than you have failed and suffered the consequences. If you don't eat all of Angie's pie you'd better not let her see that you're not man

62

enough. She don't take no prisoners!'

All this talk was very confusing for Hal, he had no idea
what it was meaning, but he did enjoy the very fine pie.
What was pressing on his mind was knowing that he was
indeed on the trail of the two men he wanted to kill, the two
men who held the key to the man behind his tragedy and
whether that man was Jim Crowley or not. They'd even
stayed here in the same saloon, so they couldn't be that far
ahead of him. Maybe he'd catch up with them before they
got to St Louis. Lost in his own thoughts he said out loud to
nobody in particular, 'How far is it to St Louis?'

'St Louis?' repeated the barkeep, overhearing him. 'You
got to get to Kansas City and take a boat down the river.
Kansas City is a good three days' ride from here and going
down river is another three or four days depending on the
boat, the captain and the number of stops he makes. I've
heard some take a week or more, and one crazy fool done it
in one day and a night and blew up his engines in the
process. Them riverboats ain't no place for a young man
from the country. Too many get into fights after losing all
their money to the pasteboard artists who swarm all over the
travellers. They're a clever bunch, will charm the money
right out of your pocket before you even lay a card. Take my
advice son, and steer well clear of them. An' don't go
chasing no dried peas under a cup, you think you see it and
then it's doggone disappeared. I don't know how they do it.'

'You seem to know quite a lot about it,' Hal remarked,
thankful for the advice.

'We get 'em in here from time to time. Travellers and
travellers' tales, men going west on the trail, men that have
lost a fortune on the boats, and some that claim to have
won a fortune, but I reckon they must've stole it. Nobody
beats them river card-sharps. Matter of fact two fellers,

ridge riders I reckon they were, passed by here yesterday, or day before. Rough lookin' fellers. Goin' to St Louis, just like you. Said they needed to win themselves ten thousand dollars, or their lives weren't worth a dime.'

'Would that be the two your wife was telling me about, Bent and Norell?'

The barkeep shook his head. 'I don't know their names, sonny. I never bother to find out their names.'

'They're in the register.'

'Don't make no difference, can't read anyways. No, I either like a man or I don't like him. I don't bother with names. I didn't like them at all. You look all right to me, make sure you keep yourself clean and we'll get along fine.'

'Clean?'

'I mean Angie. She can be a little wild at times. Gets notions into her head. Know what I'm sayin'?'

Hal shook his head, 'Not sure I do.'

'Keep it that way, son.'

'Well, I guess I'm just about done for the night anyways. Need to make an early start tomorrow if I'm to catch those two no-goods. I'll bid you goodnight, sir.'

The barkeep nodded an acknowledgement but didn't say anything more. Hal checked his pocket watch, it was near ten and he was tired from the day's ride and replete with the beef pie. It wasn't long before he was sound asleep.

Rolling over in the night he was partially awakened by a creaking of floorboards but his eyes soon closed over and sleep returned. However, he was soon awake again with the distinct feeling that someone was standing next to the bed. Cautiously he put his hand out, and making contact with another body, was instantly alert.

'Wha . . .'

A hand was gently pressed over his mouth. 'Ssshhh.

Quiet. Move over.'

Hal wasn't so green that he didn't at once realize what was happening. This was a dangerous situation. Angie was easing herself into his bed, and his first thought was not of the soft warm flesh, but her husband's words of warning. It was obviously not the first time she had done this.

'You'll get me shot,' he whispered.

'It'll be worth it,' she said, her mouth close to his ear, her hand stroking the side of his face, then smoothing his hair.

Hal dared not move, the bed would creak horribly and her husband was sure to show up with a shotgun and pepper them both more than likely. 'Your husband. . . .'

'Fast asleep, snoring like he always does. He ain't never woken up before. He ain't never woken up for anything.'

This was something of a relief, but on the other hand, wasn't exactly what Hal wanted to hear.

'You shouldn't be doing this, ma'am. You being married an' all.'

'Married? Married! You don't know the half of it. Cooped up in this god forsaken hole. Cutler's Creek. Everything creeks round here, the floorboards, the beds, the windows, my husband's bones. What does it matter? Here today, gone tomorrow. You young men, you're all the same, just out for a good time. Well, I like a good time too. Don't I deserve a good time? I even told you everything I know about those two men you're hunting. You're grateful for that, ain't you? Ain't you?'

She was starting to whine a little. Hal eased himself over to give her a bit more room in the bed. For her part, now, she didn't leave him much room metaphorically to get out of the situation. That was when fleetingly he remembered the prayer his ma had taught him about changing the things you can, and accepting the things you can't. And then the third line of the prayer about having the wisdom to know the difference between those two things. Right now he literally didn't know which way to turn. Angie was not a bad-looking woman, and she was close enough to his own flesh for him to feel the soft inviting warmth of hers. He was struggling to ignore what was patently obvious – she was stark naked and pressing ever closer.

What passed between them in the next couple of hours is not something that Hal ever divulged to anyone, besides which, as dawn was poking its fingers of light into the room, they were rudely interrupted when the door burst open and sure enough the dark form of Angie's husband was clearly apparent in the doorway. In the half-light, Hal had no idea if he was carrying a gun, but he wasn't about to take a life-changing chance on it. Leaping out of bed he rushed to the doorway and landed a crashing blow on the man's jaw. Angie screamed.

'Have you killed him?'

'No ma'am, just floored him. Now I must get goin' before he wakes up.' Hastily pulling on his longjohns and trousers, scrabbling into his shirt, and struggling with his boots, Hal collected his saddle-bags and made for the door. 'I didn't want to hit him, ma'am, but it's too late now. I thank you, Angie, for the information and everything, but I must go.'

'At least you remembered my name,' she said with a sigh, before turning over and pulling the sheets over her head with a muffled, 'Look in again, on your way back.'

Hal made all haste to the livery, collected his horse, saddled up and rode out. Cutler's Creek was somewhere he was not likely to forget, or ever visit again.

CHAPTER 7

When the early morning clouds dispersed, the sun shone brightly on the road leading eastwards in the general direction of Kansas City. The barkeep at Cutler's Saloon, Angie's husband, had said it would be a three-day ride. Hal suddenly started to chuckle. His knuckles were sore, but he bore no grudge against Angie's husband. Lashing out was an instant reaction of self preservation and he fervently hoped the sharp upper cut hadn't done any lasting damage. On reflection, the whole situation had been bizarre, worse in some ways than stories he'd heard of the ubiquitous honky-tonks found in every cowtown.

Had he behaved dishonourably? Used only to the occasional dance in a Duport saloon or a bit of fun at a celebration dinner, Hal knew little of the world away from his life as the son of a busy rancher. Of course there had been scrapes of one kind or another, childish escapades with young friends like Ben Holder, some of which had ended in a good leathering with his pa's belt. But Hal had always known it was usually deserved. His pa was never vindictive or violent, he ruled the house in much the same way as he ruled the ranch. Physical reinforcement was part and parcel of growing up, whether for boys or steers.

But when Hal was about the age of ten his pa had stopped using his belt and simply gave him a good talking. Hal grew up knowing that violence was only to be used when nothing else would do. People had to be made to see the error of their ways through dialogue, that way they might learn to be better people. However, some miscreants shouldn't be given that chance. His pa had always taught him that low-life critters had sunk that low because those good-for-nothings didn't never listen. Hal was quite clear on that point. He had no moral qualms about contemplating violence towards the murderers of his ma.

But thinking of Angie, as for meeting girls and that kind of social interaction, the opportunities in Duport were very limited. There had been the inevitable explorations of physical differences when playing with one of Ben's sisters, but every young person went through that stage of growing up. As for serious romantic attachment, Hal could count on one hand the number of girls he'd danced with at local hops. That's not to say he hadn't enjoyed it, far from it. It was exhilarating, swinging a girl round the dance floor, clasping her waist, sensing delicate feminine perfume, even having their hair flicked across his face as they swirled round and round. But there had been nothing more intimate than walking out a couple of times with the daughter of the grocery store owner, and a shared glance in church. His heart had often quickened, but had never been lost to feminine wiles. The intimate contact with Angie had been exciting, surprising, and not altogether too frightening for a greenhorn – but other things were uppermost right now.

With a careful mix of trotting, cantering and galloping, and occasional rests, Hal made good progress over the next couple of days. The road he was following passed through the odd conglomeration of wooden buildings trying to grow into townships. He stopped only briefly here and there to purchase food supplies and make casual enquiries in saloons and barber shops, giving descriptions of Brent and Norell. He was disappointed to get no new information, as they must have passed this way, or close by. Now it looked as if he wouldn't catch up with them before Kansas City, and from everything he'd heard, the maze of streets was clustered around a great trading and staging post, a massive cowtown, at the confluence of two mighty rivers. Surrounded by a spider's web of roads it was a sprawling spread of every imaginable business interspersed with saloons and hotels by the dozen. Finding Norell and Brent would be like looking for needles in a haystack.

At the end of the second day towards Kansas City, he pulled up in another little town on a crossroads where the only building of any size was the saloon, which luckily had rooms and home-cooked food on offer. Hal went in, his saddlebags over his shoulder. Silence fell on the room. There were two occupied tables, one with two men eyeing him, the other with three men engaged in a card game. An attractive young woman with long black hair and high cheek bones was behind the bar. Her dark eyes gave Hal an appraising look, which made him very uncomfortable. There was Indian blood in her, and she was stunningly beautiful. Hal nodded a greeting, then looked away so as not to stare. If she was the saloon owner's wife, he didn't want to court any more narrow escapes. Fortunately he was spoken to by a man playing cards at one of the tables. 'What can we do for you, young man?'

'Looking for a room,' Hal replied courteously. 'And a hot meal.'

'Aiyana,' the man called out to the young woman behind the bar, 'get this man to sign the register and show him to a room. Then give him some pork and beans.' He turned to Hal. 'Five dollars, pay in advance.'

Hal took some coins out of his saddlebags and put them down on the card table. The man stood up; he was well built, middle aged, perhaps late forties, early fifties. 'Much obliged, stranger. My name's Bob Mason, I own this joint. You're welcome if you're a peaceful person.'

'Pleased to make your acquaintance, Mr Mason. My name's Hal Chesterton. None more peaceful than me.'

Mason pointed to Hal's holster. 'I see you're carrying a gun.'

'I don't intend using it.'

'Keep it that way. We're a quiet town.'

The young woman came out from behind the bar counter, and without looking at Hal commanded him to follow her. The card game and conversation resumed, and none of the saloon occupants showed any more interest in the newcomer.

The solid wooden building was the only one in the little township that boasted a second floor. Hal was led up the stairs and shown into one of the four upstairs rooms.

'Aiyana's a very pretty name,' Hal remarked, surprised at his own boldness.

'It means eternal blossom,' she replied, keeping her eyes averted. 'I was born in spring.'

'It's not a name I've heard before.'

'My mother was Cherokee.'

'Was?' Hal queried.

She looked down. 'Does the room suit you?'

'Yes, very much.'

Turning to go she said, 'Your dinner will be ready shortly.'

Beguiled by her fine features and undeniable beauty,

Hal didn't want the conversation to stop. Without thinking about it, he put a restraining hand on her arm. Her eyes flashed darkly as she pulled back. Hal's impetuousness caused him acute embarrassment and he immediately let go of her.

'I don't suppose two rough-looking riders passed this way just recently, yesterday perhaps?' he asked, to cover his awkwardness.

'No,' she said. 'You're the roughest-looking rider who has stopped here in the last week.' She laughed softly and ran her fingers across the stubble on his chin. 'You need a shave!'

Tingling from the contact, Hal watched her walk back down the corridor and descend the stairs without so much as a backward glance. He stroked his chin – she was right, tomorrow morning he would see the barber before setting off. For the first time ever, he was aware of his own appearance and the impression he gave to others. She may have been teasing, but maybe not. There was clearly more to life than chasing after beef on a lonely ranch! He was looking forward to his pork and beans, especially if Aiyana was within eyesight.

Just at that moment there was a dreadful commotion downstairs. Hal could hear that some men, more than one at least, had burst into the saloon. A shot was fired into the ceiling. So much for being a peaceful place! Hal opened his door slightly to listen to the heated conversation which had just begun, not all of which was distinct, as several voices were talking at once.

'Don't you deny it. . . .'

'Put your gun up, mister, there's no call for violence, or get out of my saloon. . . .'

'Shut up, old man. Where is he?'

It was this last question which made Hal prick up his ears. Could the *he* possibly mean himself? It might, or it might just be a coincidence, either way caution was necessary. He quickly drew his gun, crept out of the room and went into another one down the corridor.

'His horse is in the livery, we've tracked him to this two-bit town and as you're the only place he could be staying, we want him now.'

To his horror, Hal heard Aiyana reply. 'He's resting in his room. If you follow me I'll show you.'

Ideas were racing through Hal's mind. Two possibilities occurred to him, firstly to ease the window and drop to the walkway roof, then down to the ground and make a run for it. The only problem with that – actually two problems – was that maybe he wouldn't get away so easily, and also he wouldn't be any the wiser as to who was pursuing him, or why. The second option was beginning to feel better. Wait for Aiyana to lead them to the room at the end of the corridor, then surprise them from behind. He had to know what was going on, or he'd be forever looking over his shoulder.

His heart had moved up very close to his throat, his ears were humming with pumping blood, and he was breathing in short sharp breaths, all the while trying to maintain his composure. What if he had miscalculated and there were more than just two of them? Supposing there were more downstairs, or waiting outside? Was this some kind of posse? What had he done that was so wrong? Then he had a sudden irrational thought – could this be Norell and Brent? Had they turned the tables, did they know he was on their trail? Could they possibly have been hiding out at Cutler's Creek, waiting to see if anyone was still chasing them, and now they'd caught him unawares?

There was no time to think any more about it, the footsteps were on the stairs, the spurs were jingling. As the party went past the door, Hal eased it ajar and cast his eye down the corridor. Yes, there were just the two of them with Aiyana. Quick, make a decision!

'Hold it right there!' Hal demanded, as he slipped out into the corridor. 'Put 'em up real high, and don't go anywhere near your guns!'

Aiyana had half opened the door to Hal's room, and now sensing danger, she took cover by the door frame. The two men, duly surprised, slowly raised their hands as they turned round to face their opponent.

'Which of you is Norell?' Hal asked calmly.

One of the men frowned. 'Norell? What you talkin' 'bout, sonny?'

'I know who you are,' said Hal, confidently. 'Well, you made a big mistake here, thinking you could take me just as easy as that.' Assuming the man who had spoken to be Norell, Hal pointed his gun at the other man. 'You must be Nickel Brent. Aiyana, go and get me some rope to tie these two up. They're wanted for cattle rustling and murder, and I intend to bring them to justice.'

'You're crazed!' said the second man.

Hal sneered. 'Yeah. Guess so. Now, do you want to tell me who you're working for, who's behind this? Who gave the order to burn our ranch, and who's got the IOU?'

'Listen, sonny,' said the first man, 'you've been eatin' crazyweed. We don't know nothing about any of that, rustlin' ranches, fires, nor nothin' like that, nor any Norell or Brent. We've been sent to rough you up a bit, that's all.'

'Why?'

'You left a saloon owner with a broken jaw, and there was something to do with his wife . . .'

Hal was suddenly deflated, relieved but confused. He lost concentration momentarily. It was a bad mistake. One of the men dropped his hand, quick as lightning, and pulled his gun. Luckily for Hal the man wasn't so fast at cocking his revolver, and as he pulled the firing pin back Hal regained focus and blasted him without hesitation. The corridor was shaken with a deafening noise and filled with gunsmoke.

Hal was quick to take control. 'Keep still, mister,' he barked to the other man whose hands quickly went back into the air.

'Take it easy, son, I ain't goin' to shoot,' he replied nervously.

As the smoke cleared, the scene came more sharply into focus, in more ways than one. It was a dreadful tableau of waxworks. Hal was standing in a braced position, his revolver still smoking. Aiyana was crouching by the doorway. One man was standing against the wall with his hands raised high, the other man was motionless on the floor, blood trickling from the side of his mouth and a bright red patch spreading across his chest. There was no movement in his limbs, his face was contorted, his heart had stopped pumping, and the blood was draining from his veins.

While the three living beings were taking in the scene, Bob Mason the owner of the joint, came up the stairs holding a shotgun in front of him. 'Don't nobody move,' he commanded. 'Or I'll blow you to kingdom come. Put your gun up, sonny, and you keep your hands up high, mister. Aiyana! Come on out of there before these two do anything silly. Get downstairs and tell Ben and Amos to come up and remove this dead'un while I think what to do with these other two miscreants. This is why we need a damn sheriff in our town, only nobody wants the job! It's left to folk like me to keep the peace.' He rounded on Hal. 'I told you you're welcome if you're peaceful, an' you said none more so. Well, you sure make a good liar, sonny. Look at this mess!'

'He drew on me, I had no intention of shooting him.'

'You ain't just shot him, you killed him.'

Bob Mason looked to the other man. 'You didn't come in too peaceful, did you? An' this is the consequence. But I ain't got no reason to hold you. You can get out of it and go back where you came from, an' don't you come back here again or I'll blast you to bits, we don't need your kind in this town.'

'Much obliged. You won't regret it,' the man said, shaking, hurrying past the shotgun and down the stairs, bumping into Ben and Amos coming up to remove the body.

Mason turned to Hal. 'I can't let you go, sonny. There's a dead man here an' I have to let the law deal with that. We ain't got no sheriff, but you'll spend the night in the jail while I figure what to do. Hand me your gun, real slow now.'

Hal did as he was commanded; this was no time to show resistance. He'd shot the man in self defence, and hope-fully Aiyana would say the same if she had seen anything. Otherwise this could be a tricky situation. Mason took Hal across the street to the unoccupied sheriff's office. He put Hal's gun on the empty desk, took him to a cell and locked the door.

'I'll send someone to get a lawman tomorrow. It's out of my hands now. There's a blanket on the pallet. And water in the jug. Aiyana will bring you some breakfast in the morning. Good night.'

It felt to Hal like the most incongruous thing for Mason

to bid him 'good night'. A short while ago he had had the prospect of a warm room, a comfortable bed, a plate of pork and beans, and the sight of a pretty young woman to serve him. Now look at it! From up to down, and all in the space of an hour. It took just a couple of strangers and a single gunshot. How life is so unpredictable. Now Hal reflected on his pa's words of wisdom, words which had sunk in without much practical application to back them up, but in this instance his pa's favourite saying now had a very meaningful resonance: *It don't matter what fate deals to you, cos life's like that, what matters is how* YOU *deal with* IT. What had happened couldn't be undone. What happened next was what mattered. But in this case, what came about was rather surprising. Settling down on his pallet Hal had no idea what was at hand.

There were footsteps on the wooden boardwalk. The door to the deserted office was pushed open and light from an oil lamp threw a sharp dagger of definition across the floor and up the wall. Hal immediately sat up.

CHAPTER 8

There was a flurry of skirts, and with a lamp in one hand and a plate of steaming food in the other, Aiyana came into view. She tried to open the cell door, shook it a couple of times, then pushed the plate of food underneath.

'I didn't want to throw this away, and Pa said I might as well bring it across to you. It would be a shame to waste it, and with you locked up I would be quite safe.'

'Safe? Your father said that?'

'Yes, who else?'

Hal frowned. 'You mean Bob Mason? I thought Bob was . . .'

'My husband?'

'Well . . .'

'Do I look that old?'

Hal was embarrassed. 'No, of course not. I just thought . . .'

'Well stop thinking and listen. I shouldn't tell you this, my pa was sworn to silence, but I think you're a good man underneath that rough exterior.'

Hal ran his hand round his chin again. 'Can you get me out of here?'

'No, I mustn't, my father insists on doing things by the

law, I daren't go against him. Listen, those two names you mentioned, Norell and Brent, those men stayed here last night and left early this morning.'

Hal's eyes lit up. 'I knew it! Did they say where they were going?'

'They talked to my father for a long time. They were up half the night playing cards. Gamblers I think . . .'

'Cattle rustlers and murderers,' Hal corrected.

'I heard them say they were on their way to St Louis. They were going to take a steamer down river from Wyandott. They made my pa swear not to say anything if anyone came looking.' She looked down, feeling disloyal. 'I shouldn't be telling you this.'

'Don't worry, nobody will find out. Did they say anything about meeting someone in St Louis.'

Aiyana thought for a moment. 'No, I don't think so, just said it was going to be a bonanza payday. Now eat your food and get some rest. I'll speak up for you tomorrow.'

'It would be more help if you could get me out of here. I'm going to lose them once they get to the river. Especially if they know I'm on their trail.'

Aiyana was sympathetic, she smiled at him with her eyes. 'The cell's locked you know. I really can't help any more. But tell me why you want to catch up with them and I'll talk to Pa.'

Hal spent a few minutes giving Aiyana brief details of the IOU, the fire, his father's plight and his mother's death, and how with the posse he'd nearly caught the rustlers near Marriton. He didn't hold out much hope of her pa letting him go – after all he'd killed a man in Bob Mason's saloon, there was a body and there were witnesses, and someone would have to answer for it. Aiyana came up very close to the bars, and Hal got up too, and went close. He put his hand through the gap and stroked the side of her face.

'Thank you,' he said.

She briefly put her hand over his, then turned and walked away. 'Good night, Hal.'

'Good night,' he replied, then grabbed the fork and greedily consumed the pork and bean stew, suddenly realizing just how hungry he had become. A cup of steaming hot coffee would have been a nice note to finish on, but he was nonetheless thankful for what he'd had. With a full belly and hoping that Aiyana would persuade her pa to let him go, preferably before calling in a lawman, he lay down on the pallet, satisfied, and covered himself with the blanket.

Cold and stiff from the unforgiving rigidity of the wooden pallet, Hal woke with the dawn chorus, long before it was time to get up. Time to get up? That was a joke. There was nothing to get up for. Nothing to do except wait for Aiyana to bring him some breakfast. He pulled the blanket closer and tried to drift away again, but found that sleep only came in short handfuls interspersed with troubling dreams of trying to catch a train that wouldn't stop, then chasing after a stagecoach that crawled along the road but could never be caught, and finally, desperately spurring a horse that would go no faster than a slow walk, and in every scene just ahead of him was a semi-naked young woman clad in no more than a diaphanous swirl of silk shift, and all the time just disappearing from sight with a tantalizing backward glance and a sparkle in her eye.

He was woken suddenly by the noisy banging of a door. Judging by the sunlight coming in through a side window the sun was well up. Maybe he had drifted off for longer than he realized. Aiyana shook the cell door again.

79

'Come on Mr Sleepyhead, breakfast is here. Shame you're not going to get that shave today. You'll have a raggedy beard by the time you get out of here. My father's going to send for a lawman, but he says it might be a day or two before he gets here to deal with you.'

'Deal with me? I don't need dealing with, Aiyana, I need to get out. Listen, I'm going to lose those murdering swine if some lawman comes here and decides to take me off somewhere for more questions or to stand trial. No jury ever convicts anyone for self-defence. You saw that idiot draw on me.'

'Yes, I know. But Pa said I had to save my breath for the lawman. This is a peaceful town and we want it to stay that way.'

'Me too,' Hal asserted vehemently. 'That's why I'm chasing these murderers. They're the kind of scum that are ruining the West. Lawless sonsofbitches who just destroy everything that we're trying to build. My pa and I had a good ranch, a good living. We're breeding cattle, strong cattle that can resist Texan ticks and the like. Then along come a bunch o' no-goods, in the pay of someone who just grabs and steals everything that hard-working folk like you and me work for, and everything gets laid to waste. Since leaving the ranch to track these scum I've seen what a great country this is, miles and miles of good grazing, stands of fine timber, rivers, good soil, flourishing crops, there's everything people need to build a good life. How would you feel if your pa's saloon got burnt down?'

'We had the same, you know. Until you white men took it away. You're still taking it whenever you can, and my people are chased and herded like the buffalo we used to hunt.'

Hal looked down, ashamed; this was something he knew

very little about. Of course he'd heard stories from his pa about Indian wars, but never had any contact with Indians – after all, they were mostly now on government reservations.

'I'm sorry. I should know better.' There was an awkward silence. 'But your father's not Indian.'

'No. Bob Mason used to be a hunter, he traded with our people, and after many years married my mother. Then soldiers came and attacked our settlement. They killed everyone they found, burnt our tents and scattered everything to the wind. I was quite young at the time so I don't remember much, but my mother was killed in a raid, and when my pa, Bob, came back from a hunting trip the settlement had been wiped out. He found me a few months later on a reservation and claimed me as his legitimate child. That's when he brought me here and set up business with the saloon. He just wants a peaceful life now. He hates disturbances.'

Hal sighed. 'I suppose that's why he's taking a hard line with me. He should have bought a farm rather than a saloon!'

'You're a threat.'

'Threat?'

'Yes. He thinks some handsome young man is going to ride into town one day and take me away.'

'So, I'm a handsome young man now?'

Aiyana blushed. 'I didn't say that!'

Hal smiled at her discomfort. 'Well, in that case, he ought to be glad to be rid of me.' There was a pause; maybe Hal was waiting for an answer. 'And what do you want, Aiyana? Do you want to be rid of me too?'

She turned away. 'Your breakfast will be getting cold.' She didn't look back.

Hal momentarily lost his appetite as he watched her go. He could just catch a brief glimpse of her as she crossed the street and disappeared into the saloon. Was she the young woman in his dream? There was a great temptation to indulge in self pity. Aiyana was a very beautiful, young, unattached woman, and his recent escapades had begun to turn his head towards the fairer sex. His heart was being pulled in more directions than he could ever remember, and it was causing him much anguish. He knew he had to trail and catch Norell and Brent, but he wanted to continue playing the game with Aiyana, who was not unresponsive in her alluringly off-hand way. He took up the plate of food and pushed it about listlessly.

'Idiot,' he said out loud to himself. 'Where's your priority, Hal my lad? Get out of this hole and catch those bastards. First things first. It was Pa's love of a woman all those years ago that seems to have brought this tragedy on us. Now look at what's happened. There's a time for everything. And right now is not the time for love making.'

He scoffed the breakfast feeling well pleased with his self admonition, and vowed to take full notice of his own advice. He expunged all thoughts of Aiyana, and began to concentrate on how he might get out of the cell. But without a key, or dynamite to blow a hole in the wall, or even something small and sharp to try picking the lock, he was at a loss. To be honest if he'd had some dynamite he wouldn't have had a clue how to use it. No, everything was hopeless, he would just have to sit it out.

That evening Aiyana brought him another hot meal, a hearty pork stew with carrots and green vegetables. She also brought some news.

'Pa sent Amos to get a lawman. There's a marshal's office a half day's ride to the north. Well, Amos got back an hour ago and said the marshal couldn't get here before tomorrow afternoon at the earliest.'

Hal turned away, dejected. The chances of catching Norell and Brent were slipping away fast. 'I might as well give up.'

'Really?' Aiyana said softly. 'You don't mean that surely?'

He shrugged. 'What else can I do? Kansas City is a big place, my chances of finding them were slim in any case. Now it could be Wyandott as well. With the trail going cold, it's hopeless.' Hal looked directly into Aiyana's eyes. A man could lose himself in those soft brown orbs.

Aiyana put her hand through the bars and touched Hal's arm then turned to go, when she reached the office door she paused and turned back. Those eyes! Hal was almost deaf to what she said.

'I'll be back for the plate. I'll bring some coffee.'

She closed the door quietly behind her. Hal tucked into the pork stew. The rich gravy was delicious, he mopped up every last drop with the corn bread. When he'd finished he pushed the plate under the cell door. What a pity he wasn't a good deal thinner or he'd have been able to wriggle out the same way. No doubt every prisoner had thought the same thing. Perhaps that's why there were never any thin prisoners in jails!

Good to her word, Aiyana returned a short while later with a cup of steaming hot coffee and his saddlebags slung casually over her shoulder. She passed the bags and the mug of coffee under the door.

'Pa said to bring your saddlebags over to you. He didn't want them left in the room in case you thought someone might take anything from them.'

'Thank you,' he said, somewhat lamely. He wanted to say so much more, even tell her about the tantalizing young woman in his dreams, but words failed him.

Almost sensing his dilemma, Aiyana said, 'Never mind about that. Life is full of twists and turns, and you never know what might happen. Sometimes we may see a brief glimpse of the future when our eyes stop looking at what we can see, and look instead at what we can feel.'

'Were you reading my thoughts?' Hal said in a surprised voice.

'Of course not. But one day, you'll remember me.' She gave him that look again, the look that the girl in his dream had given him, the enigmatic look of a young woman you can't quite read but desperately want to. She didn't give him any time to respond, leaving quickly, but turning briefly at the door, flashing her eyes at him and saying, 'Goodbye Hal, for now.'

Then she was gone, just like the girl in his dream. He pulled the saddle-bags under the door. He opened up the left side just to be sure the inner pocket still contained the gold half eagle. He'd never thought about someone stealing it, until now. The bags had been out of his possession since he was brought across to the jail, cold and dreary place that it was. He almost wished there was a sheriff in the town, one who sat smoking in his office and chatted, or played cards with prisoners through the cell bars. He put his hand into the inner pocket and felt for the little wrap of paper which contained the coin. It was there all right.

He took it out and held it in his hand. It was mesmerizing. It wasn't hard to see the attraction of gold as the little coin sat gleaming in his palm. This little piece of bright yellow metal, it had brought his pa so much happiness in winning his wife, and now so much tragedy in losing her. There was a lesson for Hal in that moment of reflection, and he knew it without really understanding the meaning.

He replaced the coin in its wrap. But what was this? In the bottom of the saddlebag, something that shouldn't be there, something that was definitely not his. A large iron key. Aiyana! God bless you, girl! So his entreaties hadn't fallen on deaf ears after all. Did her pa know what she had done? Did she do it with her pa's blessing? It didn't matter. It was a key and that was that. Excitedly, Hal fumbled it out of the bag and slipped his hand through the cell bars, but he couldn't quite align it with the lock and dropped it in the process. Luckily it didn't bounce too far away and he could just reach it with an outstretched arm.

So, Aiyana had really meant goodbye when she said it. Now all he had to do was wait until the night was older, the street was quiet, the townsfolk safely in their beds and the stars lighting his path. But what had she meant when she said for now? Did she really think he would return? He put that thought aside to wait until it was time to escape, but the image wouldn't go away, the image of the girl always just disappearing, always just out of reach. No, he must put those thoughts behind him. Norell and Brent were the focus, and he must find them before any other thoughts could be entertained. He lay down on the wooden pallet, closed his eyes and drifted away.

It seemed only a moment later that he sparked into life. He checked his pocket watch by the light of the moon – midnight had come and gone. Now was the time to make a move.

More carefully now, he felt for the front of the lock and the keyhole. It creaked slightly as he turned it and the door squealed on its hinges, but at least it was open. It took Hal less than a quarter of an hour to gather his things, remove his horse quietly from the livery yard and make haste on foot round the backs of the buildings. He paused behind the saloon and looked up at the windows. Aiyana was asleep in one of those rooms. If only he knew which one, he could thank her properly for what she had done. He sighed, bit his lip, and moved on. Safely away from the little township he mounted up, and picking his way carefully by the light of the moon, rejoined the beaten path in an easterly direction. Wyandott on the banks of the Missouri was the next destination.

CHAPTER 9

The miles slipped by without Hal noticing – he was too deep in thought to be aware of night becoming dawn or dawn becoming day. Despite it being late summer, *eternal blossom* was tugging at his heartstrings. Aiyana – what had she risked to get that key? Was she now in trouble, would she get a beating? Hal wondered how Bob Mason would respond to his daughter letting the prisoner get away, especially as he was nervous about Aiyana being whisked off her feet by a handsome young man. Had Mason really said that, or were those Aiyana's words?

Now he felt a pang of remorse at not having said goodbye properly to Aiyana, and even worse, a pang of guilt at contemplating her punishment without any chance of going to her aid. But he couldn't go back. He didn't even know the name of that two-bit town, assuming it had a name. Perhaps Masonville, since Bob Mason seemed to be the biggest noise amongst the citizenry. Well, he had ordered Amos and Ben to remove the body and they'd complied at once, and he did say it was left to him to do all the sheriff's work since there wasn't one in the town. A town without a name? No, Hal decided to think of it as Masonville, since Mason's saloon was the only building of

87

any note in that wind-blown bit of off-the-track Kansas.

Now a slight pang of hunger reminded Hal that it was time to seek out some breakfast. His supplies had all been used up except for some coffee beans. He was tempted to stop and make a fire while the sun climbed into the clear blue sky, but he'd lost enough time already and the two fugitives were gaining ground.

A fingerboard eventually pointed the way to Wyandott, and duly following the track, which at length joined a major road, the sprawling city came into view. Laid out with fine straight streets and teeming with life, livestock and industry, this was Hal's first introduction to the thriving commercial activity of an important town. Riding his horse down one of the streets he mingled with folk of every description and every background. Overwhelmed by the size and abundance of tall brick and stone buildings, several storeys high, he paused to ask directions for the river and the steam-boats. Such was the size of the place that it took another quarter of an hour of avoiding other road users, including carts and laden wagons of every description, and pedestrians careless of the dangers flitting from one side to the other, or foolishly stopping mid-street for a conversation, causing blockages and diversions at every turn.

At last the smell of the river reached Hal's nostrils. There was no doubt it was the river, as the odour intensified and the noise increased tenfold. A railway track ran along the bank, where a dozen or more steamboats in a variety of sizes and colours were at different stages of loading and unloading. The river itself was a slow-moving, murky swirl of mud and debris. A steam train had come to rest in the goods yard and was testing its boilers with immense outpourings of smoke, steam and deafening hissing noises, almost as much as the ear could stand.

Hal simply sat in the saddle casting his eye up and down wharfside, trying to fathom where to begin and how to proceed. On closer inspection he was troubled to notice that most of the boats were engaged in commercial rather than passenger activity. He would have to start asking for guidance, and the sooner the better. For no good reason he had imagined that Wyandott would be less busy than Kansas City, that if Norell and Brent had indeed come here, then tracing them might not be too difficult. Oh, the stupidity of ignorance!

By late afternoon, Hal knew he was indeed on a wild turkey chase with little prospect of catching his quarry. Exhaustive enquiries up and down the river bank and at every quayside turned up no useful information, except that he would be better advised to make his enquiries in Kansas City since more steamers plied downriver to St Louis than from Wyandott, where most of the trade was westwards upriver, garnering the agricultural and mining output of the busy hinterland as far as the Rockies.

Hal was despondent. His naivety had led him to think that all he had to do was get to the river and find the steamboat on which Norell and Brent were travelling. Of course it then occurred to Hal, those slippery characters might just have sown that seed with Mason in case he did indeed divulge their overnight stay at his saloon to their pursuer. The only sure thing was that no train line would be the least use, and so travel to St Louis by river was the only real possibility, short of riding the vast distance by horse. There was nothing to do, except go on to Kansas City, but he was tired, hungry and down-hearted. The cell in Masonville with a hot meal delivered by Aiyana, and conversation with her, seemed infinitely preferable to anything that might happen in Wyandott. Hal hadn't yet learned that such thoughts are always the prelude to something unexpected.

'Excuse me young man, I don't suppose you could tell me where the Grand Hotel is?'

Hal looked down at the enquirer. It was a little middle-aged lady with a large bonnet and grey hair. She was wearing a coat of good quality, and Hal caught sight of a glint of bright gems around the high collar of her black dress. She was carrying a furled parasol and wearing strong black boots whose heels didn't increase her small stature by much. It was plain she was as lost as he was.

'I'm afraid I don't, ma'am.'

She smiled at him. 'I was told it was one of the main streets running away from the riverside. It's a tall building and should be easy to see. Harrison Street I think it was. Oh dear, I'm so confused. Could you help me?'

Hal slipped down out of the saddle. 'I'm a stranger in town, ma'am, only just arrived myself this morning. I don't know the names of any of the streets or the names of any hotels. But I'll gladly help you. Just stick with me and I'll find a way through all these people. Here, give me your valise. We'll ask someone if they know the way.'

Resting her bag on the saddle, leading his horse, with the little lady beside him, Hal pressed through the bustle of people until they came to a less busy spot.

'I'll ask someone here,' he said. 'By the by, my name's Hal Chesterton and I'm pleased to make your acquaintance, ma'am.'

'Winifred Carmody,' she replied, holding out her hand like a dog's paw. Hal wasn't sure how to shake it when offered that way, so he just awkwardly patted the back of her hand. She smiled to herself at his obvious discomfort, this was a country boy, fresh into the city.

'Excuse me,' Hal said to the first passing man he could

stop. 'The Grand Hotel, Harrison Street?'

The man shook his head. 'Sorry, never heard of it.'

Winifred laughed a little high-pitched laugh. 'Well, he didn't know much about Wyandott, did he? One of the largest hotels and one of the busiest streets and he's never heard of them!'

With hindsight, Hal should have been alerted by her amusement. Unfortunately he was too intent on being a good Samaritan to make a proper assessment of the situation. He didn't pick up her evident familiarity with the hotel and its importance in the city. It never crossed his mind for a moment that she was the one doing the leading.

Stopping another passer-by and another until he got a sensible answer, Hal persisted until he was satisfied that the directions were adequate.

'It would be best if I walk with you, ma'am. There's a deal of folk milling about here and I'd like to see you safely to the door.'

'Oh, there's no need for that, young man, now I know that it's only four blocks down, I'm sure I can manage. I'll just go down here and take a left turn at the end.'

Hal wouldn't hear of it and insisted on staying with her. They walked on for a while without conversation, then the lady stopped and took hold of Hal's arm.

'I don't suppose you've had time to book yourself into a hotel, have you?'

'No ma'am, not yet. I wasn't planning on staying here tonight. I was hoping to get a boat down river, but nothing was going and it's getting a bit late now so . . .'

'Well, I'm sure there'll be room in the Grand, why don't you stay there?'

'The Grand sounds rather too grand for me, Miss Winifred, I'm not used to fancy hotels, fine clothes and that sort of thing. I'll find somewhere on the edge of town.'

Winifred squeezed Hal's arm and starting walking again. 'Certainly not, I won't hear of it. You've been so kind to me and you know what they say about one good deed deserving to be rewarded with another. Now, you just come along with me and I'll see you get fixed up.'

Hal had no choice but to go along with Winifred Carmody and see what happened. It wasn't too long before they turned into Harrison Street and arrived in front of the Grand Hotel. Winifred called a stable lad over and told him to take Hal's horse round to the yard, then took Hal's arm again and led him up the steps into the hotel. A uniformed flunky held the door open and raised his hat to Winifred. They went up to the desk. Winifred addressed the clerk and asked for her reservation, and for another room for Mr Chesterton. They waited while the clerk flicked through some cards. He got to the end of the pile and looked up uneasily.

'I'm sorry ma'am, but we don't seem to have a reservation for you.'

'Are you absolutely sure?'

'I'm sure ma'am. But we have an arrangement with a good little hotel in the next block and they're sure to have a couple of rooms. I'll send a boy across now to confirm it.'

He rang the desk bell, a lad appeared in a smart uniform, got his instructions and hastened off.

Winifred turned to Hal. 'Never mind. I'm sure everything will be sorted out.'

The lad returned almost before he had gone, and nodded to the clerk. The clerk in his turn nodded to Winifred and she reciprocated with a wink, visible only to the desk clerk. In a moment Hal found himself and Winifred being led across the street, down a path and to the much smaller and much less grand Bergère Hotel. The lad took them to the check-in desk. Winifred gave him a tip and off he went with a cheery *thank you ma'am.*

Very much smaller than the entrance to the Grand but in its own way a delightful hotel lobby with heavy red velvet drapes, potted plants on ornate wooden stands and gilt-framed mirrors, the Bergère was a cosy little hotel. Unusually, the desk clerk was a young woman attired some-what eccentrically in a state of semi-undress wearing just a wine-red, front-laced corset-dress and a black ostrich feather in her hair. Hal gave Winifred a questioning glance, but she simply smiled back.

'You see,' she said, 'I told you it would work out.'

'Yes, but you had a reservation at the Grand,' Hal remarked putting his saddle-bags on the desk and Winifred's valise on the floor, while he signed the register. 'This isn't quite the same, is it?'

'Never mind. We'll be just as comfortable here. Connie will show you to your room and see to all your needs.'

'My horse is still in the yard at the Grand.'

'Don't fret Hal, the lad will bring it over here. He's prob-ably already done it.'

Hal's mind was put at ease, but being inexperienced in the ways of big cities he had no idea what was really going on. Connie came round from behind the desk and Hal couldn't help noticing that what he had thought was a corset dress was in fact just a corset with a bunched tail perched on the young lady's smart posterior, revealing her long slender legs clad in patterned black stockings with satin garters. It did seem rather strange, but not something that Hal felt able to comment on. He meekly followed Connie up the stairs, three flights then down a long corri-dor. She unlocked the door and handed Hal the key. The room was sumptuously decorated, way beyond what he had expected. It made him wonder how the Grand was decorated if this was just a small out-of-the-way hotel. But then how was he to know what kind of establishment he was in?

'A very nice room,' Hal said.

'We like to look after our guests,' Connie replied. 'I'll come up after you've had dinner and see that everything's to your liking.'

'I wonder if Miss Carmody will be joining me for dinner,' Hal said, more to himself than the young lady. 'I'm rather concerned about her. She had a reservation at the Grand but the desk clerk couldn't find it. She seems rather frail and confused. Will she be all right here?'

Connie looked at Hal with wide eyes and a broad smile. 'All right here?' She laughed a tantalizing little laugh and shrugged a shoulder in Hal's direction. 'Oh, I think she'll be fine. And so will you, Mr Chesterton. So will you.' She briefly stroked Hal's arm, almost as lightly as to make him wonder if he imagined it, and made for the door. Just before she left, she turned back. 'Dinner will be ready in the dining saloon as soon as you are.'

'Thank you, Miss.'

It didn't take Hal five minutes to freshen up with a splash of water from the jug. He ran his hand round his stubbly chin. He sure did need that shave, but he kept leaving everywhere in a hurry with no time for visiting the barber. Tomorrow would be different. Whatever else happened he'd get a shave first thing before setting out for Kansas City. Right now it was time for dinner.

The dining room was as richly decorated as the rest of this hotel. The clerk at the Grand had said it was a little hotel. But Hal was on the third floor and there were lots of rooms. The dining room wasn't busy, the tables were well spaced out, and there were a number of private alcoves around the perimeter with curtains drawn and sotto voce conversation creeping out through the gaps. Hal took little notice of his surroundings, except the incongruity of all the waitresses wearing much less than would normally be expected in a smart dining saloon. He was more interested in the slab of good beef, an inch thick and tender all the way through. Not only that, he was looking forward to a proper night's sleep in a proper bed with a soft mattress to make up for that hard wooden pallet in Masonville's cell.

But he instantly changed his mind, saying to himself that he'd willingly stay on a hard wooden pallet if he could spend just ten minutes now talking with Aiyana. He imagined her sitting in the empty chair at his table for two. What would she have chosen to eat? A steak like himself, or pork ribs, maybe a meat pie, or just an omelette? What silly thoughts, he chided himself for his sentimental stupidity. Would he flip a coin now if one side won Aiyana and the other lost her for good? Would he? How had his pa taken that risk, to gamble with happiness, could he really have done that?

The rest of the meal passed by in a blur. He found himself back in his room undoing the paper wrap and taking out the half eagle. He examined it carefully, then flipped it into the air and let it fall on the floor. The eagle head was showing. He did it again and whispered to himself, *would I gamble you Aiyana on the eagle head showing?* The coin fell on the floor and rolled under the bed. Hal fell to his feet, saw the coin and pulled it out flat to preserve the heads up. As he took his finger off the coin, the eagle head stared up at him. He flipped again, and again. Every time the eagle was showing heads up. Coincidence, luck, or was something else going on?

There was a knock on the door. 'Mr Hal Chesterton? Are you in there?'

Hal opened the door. It was Winifred. 'I just wanted to check that everything was to your liking. You were so kind to help me, this is the least I could do for you. The bill has been taken care of, there'll be nothing to pay and I wish you good luck in Kansas City. Billie will be along soon to see that you have everything.'

'Oh, I have everything already, thanks. And thank you so much for your generosity.'

'As I said, one good deed deserves another. Well, I'm off to bed now, so good night.'

'Good night,' Hal said, feeling very satisfied with the outcome of his *good deed*. He closed the door. But almost as soon as it was shut, there was another knock. Hal thought perhaps Winifred had forgotten to tell him something. He opened the door.

'Hi there, Hal. My name's Billie. May I come in?' She was already leaning herself towards him and gently pushing him back.

'Billie? I thought Connie ... Oh yes, of course,' Hal replied without knowing why he was inviting this scantily clad young woman into his room. 'Everything's fine, thanks, Billie. I have everything I need.'

'Really?' Billie wondered, walking so close up to Hal's chest that he had to retreat as she gently marched him towards the bed until he fell back on to it. 'Are you quite sure?' she asked.

CHAPTER 10

It was not a position Hal was accustomed to, sprawled some-what clumsily on his back, at the edge of the bed with his feet still on the floor, and Billie standing over him with a smile that was very unsettling. The episode with the saloon owner's wife came starkly back into his mind and fixed him to the bed with a totally debilitating inertia. What was he to do? He was utterly powerless.

'Listen,' Billie said softly, her face but an inch or two away from Hal's heavy breathing. 'I need your help.'

'You need *my* help!'

'I saw you downstairs earlier in the dining room and I liked your honest face. There's something about you that gives a girl hope, lets a girl trust you to be kind.'

'Kind!' Hal blurted from his prostrate position, and it has to be said that although pinned down he could easily have pushed Billie back, but chose not to.

'Yes, that's why I asked madam if I could be the girl sent up to you tonight.'

'Why? What do you mean *sent up*, and who's madam? Explain.'

'You know very well what I mean, you teaser.'

Hal was becoming more doubtful by the minute. 'I honestly don't. If you'll let me sit up properly, I'll hear you out, and see if there's anything I can do to help you. You'd better start at the beginning or I'll lose the thread completely.'

Billie moved to one side so Hal could regain an upright position. 'Talking of threads,' she said, sitting down next to him, very close, 'perhaps you could undo that lace at the back, it's much too tight, I'm being squeezed like a marrow into a pickling jar.'

Hal stood no chance with Billie. He was just a country boy with an honest face and a complete lack of worldly wisdom.

'Thank you,' she said, 'now this one at the front.'

But Hal wasn't that green. He could see exactly what would happen if that lace was undone!

'Not yet. Tell me who is this madam and what did you mean about being sent up to me?'

'Miss Carmody of course. She's the madam, she runs the joint.'

'Winifred!' exclaimed Hal, barely able to utter the name, such was his shock.

'Of course, who else?'

'But I thought she was just a little old lady who'd lost her way and couldn't find her hotel.'

Billie smiled sideways at Hal and stroked his face. 'You poor young greenhorn! Did you really think that?'

'Well, yes I really did,' Hal said with obvious disbelief still lingering in his voice. Then he explained to Billie the circumstances of his chance meeting with Winifred Carmody, their trek to the Grand and the mix-up over the booking which led to him staying here in this hotel.

'Hotel?' Billie said, surprised. 'Men rent rooms here by

the hour. This top floor is the only one where we have guests who actually stay all night and are still here for breakfast, like you. Why, you poor fellow, didn't you know you're staying in the smartest whorehouse this side of the Missouri?'

Hal was speechless. The two of them sat side by side for several minutes without a word passing between them. Hal looked quite dejected with his head slightly bowed as if he'd stupidly been caught stealing a pie from the kitchen. Billie put her arm round his shoulder and pulled him close.

'Oh dear me,' she said, ever so softly. 'Poor country boy taken in by a little old lady. In the morning, you'd be presented with a massive bill. We're expensive, you know, and you've got me all night. And if you couldn't pay it, the city police would be called and you'd be locked up. Then Miss Carmody would come and visit you in the cell, and offer you the chance to pay off the debt by doing a job for her.'

'Well, I certainly haven't got much money with me. Anyway, Winifred said my bill was taken care of. What sort of a job?'

'Robbery, a hold-up, an assassination, something significant. That's why I want out.'

'What do you mean, *out*?'

'That's how you're going to help me. Now do you want to undo this lace?'

Hal hesitated. Well, who wouldn't? But he didn't move. 'Tell me how I can help.'

'I hate this life. I'm a rabbit in a trap. Oh yes, it was fun at first, all the admiration, the attention, the gifts. I even got a share of the takings for a couple of months, but soon the debts started mounting up. Clothes, laundry, food, lodging, eventually every girl realizes there's no way out of this life until the debt is paid, and it just keeps getting bigger.

Madam has complete control. She has men to track down any girls who try to leave, some never come back, they get free, but they didn't really escape, they ended up in a ditch or in the river.'

'Why don't you go to the police or the marshal's office?'

'Impossible, they're all clients.'

'So how do you propose I can prevent you ending up in the river?'

'It's simple. We leave in the middle of the night and you take me far away where I can't be traced.'

'But she knows my name and will no doubt send people after me, too.'

'We could set fire to the place and it would be a long time before they knew who was dead or alive.'

'Absolutely not,' said Hal emphatically. 'Innocent lives would be lost. You can't control fire.' The horror of what his mother must have suffered flashed back into his mind. He stood up angrily. 'I don't want to be part of anything like that. I think you'd better leave now.'

Billie didn't get up. She patted the bed beside her. 'Don't take off so. You don't mean that.'

'I do.'

'You don't want to die, surely?'

'Die?'

Billie smiled, but not in a nice way. 'I only have to raise the alarm and say you've been beating me. There's half a dozen men look after this building you know, all armed and ready to kill if there's any trouble. Madam runs a very tight ship here. Now, sit down and listen.'

Hal sat down reluctantly.

Billie continued. 'We can easily get away down the fire escape. I've got it all worked out, believe me. I've been planning this for a couple months, just waiting for the right kind of man to come along and help me. I only get one chance at this, if it fails I'm dead.' She paused to let the implication sink in.

'I don't like it, you know. Tell me why I should put my life in danger for you.'

Billie's fingers went to the lace and slipped it out of the top two eyes. Hal grabbed her hand to stop her going any further. Billie pouted.

'I'm serious,' he said. 'Tell me why.'

'For the same reason you helped Miss Carmody, when she seemed lost and vulnerable. I am too. I don't want this life, there's something better, I know it, I'm prepared to risk death to find that something. Won't you help me?' She got up and turned back the sheets. 'We only have to wait a few hours until well after midnight, everybody has either gone home or gone to bed by then, and there's just a few hours before everything starts to wake up, that's our best chance. Now what shall we do to pass the time?'

For the second time that night Hal found himself in an unfamiliar position. It was three o'clock in the morning, very dark and very quiet. The fire escape had stopped some eight feet short of the ground, but luckily Billie was not heavy boned and she'd dropped easily into Hal's arms. A small bribe for the stable lad had secured his horse from the yard at the Grand. Now with Billie riding pillion behind him, he took the narrowest and most deserted streets with the least amount of lighting. He had told the lad he was going south, which was true, thinking that when questioned, as would be inevitable by Winifred's men, they would think he'd tried to lay a false trail and would go every other way but south. Well, it might work. As for his actual intention, once he'd cleared the city limits and his heart had resumed a normal beat he told Billie to hold on tight. He spurred his horse into an easy canter to eat the miles as quickly as possible. Dawn hadn't broken when they arrived in the outskirts of Kansas City, but as the sun came up Hal lost no time in enquiring at the wharf for a steamboat going downriver that day.

'You're not going to leave me here in Kansas City, are you, Hal? I've got some money, just a few dollars, but it's not enough to get me anywhere safe.'

'What do you propose?'

Billie put her hands on her hips. 'Well, you could take me with you. You're going to St Louis aren't you, so you could put me on a train there for Chicago or New York. Boston's quite smart, so I've heard.'

'I've no idea if you can get trains to those places . . .'

'So let's find out.'

It was pointless carrying on this banter. Hal knew he would be beaten at every turn. Billie was not a country girl, she was smart, might even have been to school, and could read and write. He had no choice but to give in.

'All right,' he said, 'we'll find a boat first, then breakfast. I need some good strong coffee to give me the strength to do battle with you the way you challenge everything I say.'

Billie smiled to herself, nestled her chin closer to Hal's ear and squeezed her arms round his middle even tighter. 'It doesn't have to be a battle, you know. . . .'

Hal shook his head, unlocked her hands from his stomach and slipped down off the horse. Billie moved into the saddle and walked the horse alongside Hal while he continued asking after a steamboat. Success came at last in the wharfside office of the *Kansas Star*. The clerk was pleased to tell Hal the boat – which he guaranteed was one of the best and most reliable on the river – was due to set off at midday and if Hal cared to buy a ticket he could have an excellent berth for the four day journey. This presented Hal with a brief dilemma, not for the price of the ticket, but how was he to introduce his travelling companion, and there was only one horse? Hal looked out through the office door, Billie was astride his horse on the quayside. He waved to her and she waved back.

The clerk noticed. He smiled ingratiatingly. 'You're hesitating, sir. Let me assure you, you won't find a more comfortable accommodation. . . .'

'I'll take two passenger tickets and one horse,' Hal said to cut the clerk from further persuasions.

'Excellent!' the clerk beamed. He took up his pen and dipped it in the inkwell. 'May I have your name, sir?'

'Chesterton,' Hal said openly. 'Mr Hal Chesterton.'

The clerk wrote on a ticket and then into a register. 'And is that Mrs Chesterton on the horse outside?'

'Mrs Chesterton?'

'Your wife, sir?'

'Oh no,' said Hal, suddenly shocked. 'She's not my wife.' His natural honesty was affronted, but instantly he wished he hadn't introduced such a complication. He grimaced at his dilemma.

'Indeed, sir? What name shall I put on the ticket?'

What name indeed? Who was this young woman that Hal had plucked from the thrall of a madam and risked his life to spirit way from a Wyandott whorehouse? Hal drummed his fingers on the clerk's desk with obvious indecision. The only name that came quickly to mind was Aiyana Mason. Mason? Aiyana? But which? Quick thinking came to his aid.

'My sister's name is Maisie. Miss Maisie Chesterton.'

The clerk wrote, and Hal breathed a sigh of relief, but

his ordeal wasn't over yet, and the clerk had a knowing glint in his eye.

'Would sir prefer single berths? Two singles are more expensive than a double berth. Or will you share accommodation with your sister?'

'We'll share,' Hal said quickly, in order to be quit of this interrogation, which was fast becoming worse than answering Sheriff Skeeter's questions in the jail at Marriton. Hal left the steamboat office somewhat flustered. He smiled at Billie. 'Breakfast time, Maisie.'

Her quizzical look demanded an explanation, and between the quayside and a nearby saloon advertising good home cooking, Hal tried as best as he could to explain why Billie now had a *Kansas Star* ticket for Miss Maisie Chesterton, and would be in a shared room with her brother. Hal's embarrassment was greeted by Billie's peels of delighted laughter.

'You see!' she exclaimed. 'I knew you were a good'un. The moment I clapped eyes on you in the dining room last night – was it only last night! – I said to myself, Billie I said, there's your ticket to freedom. And now look, I really have the ticket and, what's more, a new name into the bargain!'

For a moment, Hal was also pleased with the outcome. He liked to see people happy as a result of something he'd done for them, it was a good feeling. But it didn't last long. He was remembering how he'd come up with the name Maisie, and the beautiful young lady he'd been thinking about. What would he give to be travelling with Aiyana? Aiyana as Mrs Hal Chesterton. Oh yes, he liked the sound of that very much.

Billie leant across the breakfast table and put her hand on Hal's as he was about to lift a slice of hickory-smoked pork to his mouth. 'Four days and four long nights,' she said with a lovely smile, her head slightly cocked to one side.

It was a bitter-sweet thought for Hal. Under other circumstances, he would have been thrilled. No irate husband to send bad guys after him, well, maybe an irate madam's sidekicks, but they couldn't catch him on the river. Four peaceful days in the company of a very keen and not unattractive young lady – but the long nights were a different matter. He strangely felt he would be dishonouring Aiyana to succumb to the delights of Billie – Miss Maisie Chesterton. Maybe he could convince her that they had to play the part of brother and sister at all times, even during the night? Or maybe he could stay up all night and play cards in the gambling saloon, then sleep during most of the day? No, that wouldn't work, wasn't it Aiyana's pa Bob Mason who'd warned him off gambling with the riverboat pasteboard artists? Thieves and robbers every one of them. Besides which, it was gambling, and that brought to mind the gold half eagle which was at the root of all this tragedy. As things turned out, Hal need not have fretted over this small problem which would soon find its own solution.

The *Kansas Star* duly slipped its ropes and cast off just after midday. It was a wonderful sight that drew a crowd of onlookers – relatives, friends and bystanders. There was much waving, shouting, a few tears, lots of smoke and a violent thrashing of the great paddle as the boat moved slowly into the mainstream of the great muddy river. Branches, sundry debris and a dead dog floated by the steamer as it gradually picked up speed and began its long journey down the Missouri to St Louis.

A riverboat is full of the whole panoply of humankind, and when Maisie was introduced to other travellers at dinner that first evening as Hal's sister, he found that she was suddenly a honeypot. With her wide eyes, alluring attire and innocent expression, the riverboat bears began to circle round 'Miss Maisie Chesterton'. While taking coffee on deck, Billie excused herself for a moment, but failed to return for more than half an hour. Later that evening in their cabin, Hal was washing his face and hands at the washstand wondering what was to happen next, when matters were delightfully taken out of his control.

'Hal, you're a wonderful man,' she began, and Hal was immediately suspicious. 'I owe everything to you. But I recognize that a girl can only presume on so much kindness for a short time. You have been so good to me. . . .'

'What do you want to say, Billie? Get on with it.'

'You know I said I wanted to go to New York or Boston . . .'

'Yes.'

'Well, you remember Mr Ascot van Dinkel, who was sitting opposite us at dinner? He's going to Boston on business, and he's offered to take me with him, even buy my ticket!'

'Van Dinkel, the old man with short white hair and that neat little white beard? The one with little ratty eyes?'

'He isn't old, and he hasn't got ratty eyes! He owns a mine in the Rockies. Anyway, he's offered to take me with him.' She paused and fiddled with her nails, as if she hadn't quite said everything yet.

'And . . .'

Billie smiled sweetly. 'And he's got a state room on the upper deck and he wants me to spend the journey with him. Oh Hal, would you mind?'

The gods be praised, Hal thought. 'Well, Billie, I have to say you're a sly one. You were only gone half an hour! Of course I don't mind. I just hope Mr van Dinkel is as sincere as you think, and doesn't yet realize you're the one who's digging for gold.'

'He's got a silver mine, actually. He's sincere all right, look, he's given me this little wad of notes already! I want to pay you for my expenses, the ticket and everything.' She peeled off a few of the bank bills and gave them to Hal.

'I don't need all that,' he said. But before he could hand them back, she'd gathered up her things, kissed him on the cheek, and closed the door quietly behind her. Well, she'd burst into his life through his *hotel* door, now she'd breezed out of his life through his cabin door. Doors open and close. Easy come, easy go.

Instead of going to bed, Hal sat on the edge of it and reflected on the crazy events of the past forty-eight hours. Nothing could have prepared him for what life was throwing in his path. When he hot-headedly decided to take off after Norell and Brent he never imagined that fateful meeting in the two-bit town he liked to call Masonville, nor running across Miss Carmody – though on further consideration he decided she had actually run across him, deliberately. Then being alerted to the danger and rescued by Billie, and in turn rescuing her, and now it was all as if nothing at all had happened.

Here he was, alone, on a steamboat, exactly as he knew he would be, on his way to St Louis. He couldn't cope with trying to fathom out anything more right now, so he decided to go up and watch the card players at their games. Maybe he'd see how their fabled cheating was done. He spruced himself up, polished his boots, brushed his hair and put his two hundred dollars from Billie in his jacket pocket. It seemed that fate had some fresh, but not uninteresting hurdle in store for him at every turn. So far, he'd crossed every one. But he knew the biggest was yet to come, finding those two sonsofbitches and the man they were working for. Getting up, he breathed a huge, slightly despairing sigh, wondering what life would throw at him next – but as he crossed to the door, there came a knock from outside.

'Mr Chesterton? Cabin service.'

Hal pondered, he hadn't ordered anything. He opened the door and was immediately pushed back on to the bed staring into the barrel end of a revolver.

CHAPTER 11

There was nothing to be done about it. Hal was sprawled on his back with his feet still on the floor. A position that was becoming too familiar. The gunman had caught him completely by surprise, and except to wait and see what the stranger wanted, Hal was totally at a loss.

'All right, Mister Clever-guy, there's two ways out of this for you. Do as I say and you'll come to no harm, or try to protect the whore and I'll break both your legs. You're lucky Miss Carmody took a shine to you, country boy. She said I was to let you go on your way, once I've got the girl. Billie is a special kind of girl, you see. Means a lot to Miss Carmody, does Billie. So where is she?'

Trying to take in the information and fathom its meaning, Hal tried to ease himself up on to his elbow, but the gunman pushed him back down with the barrel of his gun pressing on Hal's forehead.

'Listen, mister,' Hal began, shaking his head, 'your guess is as good as mine.'

The gun barrel was pressed harder into Hal's forehead. 'Don't mess with me,' the gunman threatened. 'She's on this boat with you. You bought her a ticket in the name of Maisie Chesterton and she's staying in this cabin with you.'

'No, no she isn't,' Hal asserted angrily. 'You're wrong. She should be staying with me, but she's gone off with some other guy.'

'Yeah, yeah.'

'You can look around the cabin, there's nothing here that belongs to Billie. Nothing.'

While he cast his eye round the room, the gunman eased the pressure on Hal's forehead, although it still felt like there was something pressing into his brain.

'So where's she gone?'

'I don't know . . .'

In pure frustration the gunman smacked his knuckles into Hal's jaw, the barrel of the gun cutting him just above the eye. A trickle of blood ran down Hal's cheek.

'That won't help you find her,' Hal said defiantly.

'Miss Carmody said not to kill you, otherwise you're a dead man, Chesterton. Keep your head down and keep outta my way or you'll have a fatal accident and Miss Carmody won't shed more than two tears when I tell her why.'

Then he was gone almost as suddenly as he had appeared. Hal's self-imposed task of getting Billie to safety had taken a turn for the worse. But why? Why did he care a fig for Billie, she was nothing to him. He was glad to be shot of her, delighted that ratty-eyed van Dinkel had taken her off his hands. But now both Billie and van Dinkel were in grave danger. The gunman was determined to take Billie back to the Wyandott whorehouse, and it was quite obvious van Dinkel was entirely disposable.

Hal drew his gun, broke the cylinder and checked that all six chambers were loaded. He snapped the barrel back, spinning the cylinder and slid it into his holster. He got up and quietly closed the door behind him. Up the stairs, he pushed through the swing doors and walked out on to the deck. It was cold. The wind had a sharp, keen edge, the sky was clear, myriad stars sparkled above him, and the brightness of the moon threw heavy black shadows across the planks. Here and there a pair of nightbirds leant against the rail in an embrace against the chill. There was a surprising number of strollers at this hour still perambulating the deck, trying to walk off the effects of too much drink or settling the consequence of dining on too much rich beef, plates of vegetables and sweetmeats plastered with lashings of cream.

Hal walked to the front and leant over the side to watch the steamboat split the moonlit water like a shattered mirror, sending ripples of light and dark down the length of the boat as the bow ploughed a furrow. Somehow his life was a little like what he was watching. The undulating surface of life's ebb and flow, suddenly churned asunder by the relentless thrashing of some uncontrollable event. It starts with a gentle warning, the prow of the boat pushing aside the slow pattern of daily life, and then all hell is let loose as the giant paddle stirs up mud, debris and tranquillity into an unholy turbulence from which nothing escapes unscathed. Just so, this whole saga started with the blocking of a small tributary river on the ranch, followed by the disturbing tale of the IOU, and eventually the life-changing conflagration which left the blackened debris of a peaceful existence utterly destroyed. But there was no point in feeling sorry for himself. Hal went back into the gaming saloon and his melancholy mood disappeared in the intensity of the febrile atmosphere. Excitement and dejection hung on the turn of a card or the roll of the dice.

Looking right down the saloon, as far as he could see, the tables were full of players. Standing behind many of the tables were ladies in an assortment of fine clothes, expensive fabrics and chic styles, others less so, and some downright plain. Some were wives, some were looking to become wives, some were encouraging the players, and others were waiting to employ their feminine charms and inveigle a winner to take her back to his cabin, where, in the morning, he would find his winnings somewhat diminished and his erstwhile paramour impossible to find.

Suddenly remembering his predicament, he scanned the tables for an older man with white hair, a neatly trimmed white beard and ratty eyes. Mr van Dinkel was playing cards, and there close behind him, standing, watching the game, was Billie. Hal desperately tried to remember what the gunman was wearing, but he couldn't see anyone that looked like his vague recollection. He walked down the saloon and took up a position a little distance away so he could observe the play at van Dinkel's table and keep an eye out for the gunman. Never having played poker, believing it to be the game in progress, Hal watched cards being dealt. Corners were carefully lifted by some players, or cards picked up and held close to the chest in a tight fan so only the possessor could view the hand. Soon, coins and notes began to pile up in front of each player.

But van Dinkel never touched his cards, nor for one moment took his eyes off the other players. Sometimes he laid out a pile of dollar bills of varying denominations, sometimes he simply passed his hand palm downwards over the cards to take no further part in that hand. What intrigued Hal was that van Dinkel won more times than he lost, and all without ever looking at his cards until the reveal. It was a strange way of playing. What was the point of playing at card games if you never looked at the cards?

This poker was a strange game indeed, with the deal

being over in moments and the betting going on for com-
paratively ages. As curious as was van Dinkel's method of
play, it began to arouse the enmity of the other participants.
Hal knew very well that Bob Mason had warned Hal not to
engage with the riverboat cardsharps, but he couldn't see
how van Dinkel was cheating, if indeed he was. The more
Hal watched, the more he understood, not about the game
but about van Dinkel and his method of play. It was nothing
to do with cheating, it was purely psychological. Hal could
see how van Dinkel was riling his opponents, aggravating
them with his calm demeanour, with his apparent indiffer-
ence to both winning and losing, how he was silently luring
them into making mistakes and throwing in when maybe
they had a winning hand.

It was soon abundantly clear to Hal that van Dinkel
didn't play poker for the fun of the game or for any interest in the cards themselves, nor indeed, it seemed, in
actually winning. No, van Dinkel was simply interested in
human frailties and insecurities, in beating opponents into
submission without the least hint of violence. Van Dinkel
was playing with his mind, not his cards. It had been that
simple to lure Billie away from Hal, it had taken only a half
hour of chat it seemed. What had he promised Billie? Did
he really intend to take her to Boston, to pay for her
passage and all that? Or was this just a bit of psychological
fun, another kind of game?

Suddenly, Hal felt inexplicably protective towards Billie.
Having rescued her from the Wyandott whorehouse and
taken her to Kansas City, he'd given her up rather easily.
Supposing van Dinkel's intentions were far from honourable? Hal smiled to himself and chuckled – as if Billie
couldn't look after herself! What on earth was he thinking?
Then he remembered the gunman. Billie would be no

match for him.

When van Dinkel collected up all his winnings and carefully placed them in his inner pockets, where the notes bulged rather alarmingly, it was clear they were turning in for the night. Hal would have to follow extremely carefully. He looked round to see if anyone else was interested in following Billie and Mr Moneybags van Dinkel. There was no obvious sign of a pursuer, so Hal waited until they were near the stairway before following.

Gaining the top of the stairs Hal could see the two lovebirds locked arm in arm walking towards the luxurious bank of top deck cabins, and almost at the same instant, ahead in the half-light he saw a figure partly hidden by the shadow of a stanchion. Hal felt for the gun in his holster. He quietly pulled back the firing pin and dodged into the shadows of a doorway. Van Dinkel stopped and fumbled in his pocket for a key. A moment later, the door was pushed open. Despite his diminutive size, van Dinkel scooped Billie into his arms and carried her inside. The gunman made his move, and as soon as the laughing pair were inside the cabin, the shadowy figure had leapt forward with a drawn gun and used his boot to prevent the door from being closed.

'Easy now, you slimy old goat,' said the shadow. 'Put your hands in the air, and get away from the door. I'm coming in to settle some business.'

A calm voice replied, 'We have no business, mister, so be on your way.'

Hal thought it a very brave response, unless van Dinkel had also drawn a weapon. In that case there might be gunplay, and anyone, including Billie, might get hurt. One thing Hal had learned was not to rush in before he had a proper grasp of the situation, which in this case meant at least one man armed with a drawn weapon and not afraid to use it. The door opened wider as the gunman went in, pushing the door behind him, which remained slightly ajar. Hal took the opportunity and crept closer. His heart was beginning to race, but he checked its beat by taking deep, slow breaths.

A whole gamut of scenarios raced through his mind, not the least of which included a bad outcome for everyone. Why did he bother one way or the other? He didn't want Billie, didn't need the encumbrance, or her romantic notions, which interfered with his thoughts of Aiyana. He could just walk away, take no further notice, let things take their course. But something impelled him to stay.

'Well, Billie, thought you'd got away did you?'

'You've got the wrong woman.' It was van Dinkel speaking. 'This is Maisie Chesterton, and she's travelling to Boston with me. Her brother's also travelling on this boat. Find him and get him to confirm that, if you don't believe me.'

'Oh yes, he's on the boat all right, you old goat. I've already had the pleasure of a little chat with him. I've been tracking Billie and her brother, right here on to this boat. You don't need to be involved Mr Whatever-your-name. Just step aside and let me take Billie.'

'I will do no such thing, sir,' said van Dinkel, in a very calm and measured voice. 'Tell me what Maisie has done, and I'll consider how best to help. After all, you can't just expect me to step aside and give up my bride.'

'Your bride!' exclaimed the gunman.

But Hal could see that van Dinkel was buying time while he was puzzling what to do, trying to confuse Miss Carmody's henchman into talking and thinking, something which van Dinkel knew the gunman would be very poor at doing.

Van Dinkel continued. 'Look, mister, I have plenty of money in my pocket, how much will it take for you to leave us alone?'

'It's not your money I'm after, it's the girl. I want the girl.'

Now Hal could also see the dangerous side. The gunman was likely to lose patience at being outwitted by talk and prevarication, and might just shoot first and ask questions later – his kind operated on a short fuse. Since van Dinkel had mentioned the money, which the gunman probably knew about since he must have been watching them in the saloon, van Dinkel was in danger of being killed for a handsome sum of ready cash. Hal wasn't sure what was going through the gunman's mind, had no idea how van Dinkel planned to resolve the situation, but suddenly became very clear about what his own course of action should be. The door being slightly ajar, offering easy access, clinched it.

Hal slid the cocked pistol out of the holster, mustered his courage and gave the door a hefty shove. Standing just inside the door the gunman was knocked sharply in the back, causing him to loose off a wild shot which smashed into the wardrobe, showering van Dinkel with a shattered mirror. In the simultaneous act of pulling a gambler's derringer from his inside pocket, van Dinkel fell to the floor. The gunman turned on Hal, his revolver swinging into line, but Hal was ready and aimed a shot into the man's chest. He was thrown back across the bed and fell on the far side. Hal was on him in a flash, his gun cocked ready for a second shot. But none was needed. The man's eyes rolled briefly, then stopped in a ghastly stare, his mouth fell open and blood ran down his chin into a pool on the floorboards, then that too, stopped.

The smoke cleared slowly, but the noise took much

longer to disappear from their ears. Billie was cradling van Dinkel, who had taken a nasty cut to the head. Blood was all over his face, but then heads bleed a lot because of the veins running so close to the surface. His injuries were not life-threatening. He was moaning, but conscious, and Billie was mopping him up with a cloth and some water. She turned to Hal.

'You seem to court disaster wherever you go.'

'Me!' said Hal astonished.

'Yes, you.'

Hal shook his head. 'He was going to take you back to Wyandott.'

'Yes, I know. He was the one man I didn't want to see. He would never have given up until he had me back in that place.'

'Are you that special?'

'To him, yes. But don't shed a tear for him, the bastard, he's the one killed two of my friends who tried to get away. Carmody sent him and another man to bring them back, but he killed them. I know he killed them because I was there. He shot them both as a warning to me. It was because I went with them, I planned it, you see. That was the mistake. He'd always warned me what would happen if I tried to escape, and when he caught us he . . .'

'But he didn't kill you.'

'No. He would never have killed me, I was his toy.'

There was a long silence while Hal took it in.

She turned away from him. 'He's my father.'

Hal was pole-axed, dumb-struck. He stood there in a haze while Billie calmly went on attending to van Dinkel. She lived in an entirely different world from his. He reflected on his own father, his own dear pa and what he had now suffered. It was outside his comprehension that a daughter could be so indifferent to her father's demise, shot to death in front of her own eyes. But then, how could a father keep his daughter in captivity and make her do what Billie had to do every day? It was all part of the wide world he didn't yet know, and didn't want to.

When at last he found his tongue Hal asked almost casually, 'What now?'

'Drop him quietly over the side.'

Hal frowned in disbelief. 'I can't do that.'

Billie stopped what she was doing and looked Hal in the eye. 'If I told you about the things he did to me, his own daughter, you would probably want to put another bullet in his skull even while he's lying here already dead. Drop the bastard over the side.'

The remaining three days and nights, steaming downriver, passed without further incident. Van Dinkel, Billie and Hal took their meals together and had a fine old time of it. Van Dinkel provided the best wine the boat's quartermaster had in his store, and they dined like the president, as befitted the two occupants of the best stateroom on the boat. Hal even learnt to play poker by watching the games, then joining in. But he didn't play on the same table as van Dinkel, although he did play with van Dinkel's dollars, and he did always look at his cards before deciding what to do.

Dinner together on their last night was a bitter-sweet occasion. Billie was delightful company, she was under no illusions about the delicacy of her position and its insecurity, but van Dinkel seemed a genuine man and Eros had certainly shot him good and proper through the heart. Billie reminded him more than once he'd called her his bride!

'Well, Hal,' van Dinkel said, raising his glass. 'I wish you success in your endeavour, and when you've achieved what you want, there'll always be a job for you in one of my enterprises.'

'I don't think I'll ever be going to Boston,' Hal replied.

'Not just Boston, everywhere from Kansas to New York. Anyways it's a commercial bank in Boston, you wouldn't want to work in a bank. You're an outdoor sort of person, I've got a vacancy for a mine manager in the Rockies, or a transport manager in Lawrence, good money you know. You could settle down with a pretty young girl and make something of your life.'

Hal smiled to himself, it was worth a thought maybe. He certainly had a pretty girl in mind. But he also had a herd of beef, a severely disabled pa, and an unfinished mission. He wasn't ready to make any decisions about anything else just yet. He raised his glass.

'To Mr and Mrs van Dinkel,' he said with a broad grin.

CHAPTER 12

Now the hunt had to start in earnest. Van Dinkel and Billie had been good fun in so many ways, and the river journey had been both exciting and adventurous, but for Hal, arrival in St Louis marked the start of a serious challenge. He had to push all the joviality of the last few days to the back of his mind and figure how to begin his search for these two needles in this haystack of St Louis. Where to begin? It was probable that every steamboat issued tickets with names on, maybe he could check the registers of any boats which had come in over the last couple of days. It would be a place to start and something to get him going. But walking along the quayside it didn't take him long to realize that checking every boat that had arrived from Wyandott and Kansas City over the last few days was a task beyond one man working alone, and every minute lost made the hunt more difficult. He sat down on an iron bollard and stared into the murky water slapping against the quay.

So, Norell and Brent were meeting Mr Big in St Louis. Where would they meet him? In a hotel? In Mr Big's office – would he have an office in St Louis? And why did he think this main man was a Mr Big, it could be just plain old Jim

Crowley, if indeed Jim Crowley was the man behind this tragedy. Jim Crowley – yes, he had to be playing a part in this – after all, he was the one in possession of his pa's IOU, and the prisoner in the cell had said they were meeting Mr C in St Louis. At the end of a good deal of puzzling, Hal felt he was no nearer the answer. Dejected, his mind wandered away from fugitives and for a moment a warm glow spread through his body as Aiyana began to replace the other thoughts.

'Move on, mister. You're in the way, some folk have got work to do. There's nothing here for you.'

Hal looked up, surprised. A dockhand was glaring down at him with a rope in his hand. Hal hadn't even noticed a packet boat coming alongside the wharf. He got up quickly and stepped back. The man had caught the end of a light rope and began pulling it in. It was attached to a much larger rope which he proceeded to haul in and then wound round the bollard. Hal watched, fascinated at the man's skilfully precise movements, not wasting an ounce of effort and seemingly with apparent ease pulling this huge steamer alongside, not quite single-handed, there being two other men doing the same along the wharf, but human muscle power controlling so many tons of shipping with just simple ropes, thick as a man's arm, but rope nevertheless.

Then suddenly everything became clear. Firstly, van Dinkel's lessons in psychology, and now this simple example of how easy it is to manipulate an almost immovable object given the right conditions. Hal's mind had been ripe for the sowing of seeds. A man hell-bent on a particular mission is as immovable as this steamboat, but with a small piece of rope it's as tame as a pet dog.

What exactly was Hal doing here in St Louis? He was focused on catching Norell and Brent. How did he know they were here? Because Aiyana had said she'd heard they were going to Wyandott to get to St Louis for a bonanza payday. What a fool he'd been. He never thought Norell was very smart, but now it looked as if Hal himself was the one who'd been taken in with such a simple deception. Norell had told Mason they were travelling under false names, but let him also know their real names, then said they were being followed and were going to St Louis. Oh so neat! Norell had laid a clever trail to get Hal out of the way, making sure everyone in Bob Mason's saloon had also overheard all the details. Now Hal was sitting on the dockside in St Louis like a total tinhorn, further away from Norell and Brent than ever.

So what were Norell and Brent up to? Hal pondered for a moment more objectively. What a fool he was – they didn't have the cattle and they didn't have ten thousand dollars. There wasn't any payday for them, they'd failed in their task. In fact they wouldn't be able to show their faces to Mr Big until they had something to show for their efforts. The question was, did Mr Big just want the ten thousand dollars of the IOU, or was there more to it than that? Was Jim Crowley really the Mr Big behind this, and if so, had he fallen on hard times and was after money, or had he actually intended some kind of revenge against Hal's pa? It didn't yet make any sense however he looked at it.

Nothing would be resolved without catching up with Norell and Brent. Maybe they were just sidekicks, but they were the only people who might have some answers. Either way it now seemed like a good idea to go back to Masonville and talk to Bob Mason. His heart was gladdened at the thought of seeing Aiyana again. But, wait – it was Aiyana who had fed him all the information about Norell and Brent, about them signing false names, about saying someone was following them, about their immediate plans. She'd overheard all this in the saloon, like everyone else. Surely she hadn't deliberately misled him, been told to give him the false information? It was Aiyana who had helped him to escape, sent him on his way to Wyandott for a river-boat to St Louis. He began to feel it was her fault he was here on the dock wondering what to do next.

However hard he tried to push those thoughts to the back of his mind, they wouldn't go away. A seed of doubt had been sown into the virgin soil and he didn't want it to grow. The only possible solution was to go back home to Duport and start all over again. He now saw he'd been too keen to take off after the rustlers and just chase blindly without stopping to think. Most animals that run when pursued, are keen to seek cover or some other means of shaking off their pursuer. The trail Hal was following had certainly led from Marriton to Masonville, but he'd allowed himself to believe it went on to St Louis because he trusted the person who had given him the information. In his eyes, Aiyana could do no wrong, maybe that was his fundamental mistake. And now he didn't want to go back to Duport empty-handed, he didn't want to turn up in his home town looking as if the task had beaten him, nor try to explain what had gone wrong without implicating and besmirching Aiyana – something he absolutely wouldn't do.

There was one other course of action, and that would be to go back to Marriton and look for a trail that might lead to Jim Crowley. For the moment at least, the trail on Norell and Brent could be abandoned. Jim Crowley was now the target.

The prospect of another river trip, maybe this time six or seven days against the current, did not fill Hal with plea-sure. But then with plenty of van Dinkel's dollars still in his pocket maybe there was some fun to be had. Maybe it would take his mind off Aiyana for a few days. In the same way that van Dinkel met Billie by chance, maybe Hal, too, might meet a vivacious, unattached young lady. Now that he'd got used to having company, several days alone seemed rather dull.

He made his way along the dockside and eventually found a boat with a suitably comfortable berth leaving that very afternoon. Pocketing his ticket Hal had to laugh at himself – not many days ago he was more than content to sleep in his bedroll under the stars in a clear Kansas sky. Now he was choosing a comfortable cabin all to himself for a bit of fun on a steamer with a proper restaurant and gaming saloon. His pa would be scornful if he did but know! *God bless you Pa*, said Hal out loud. *Don't you worry, I'm still on the trail.*

It would be a deception to pretend that Hal enjoyed the journey. He passed the time in conversation with other travellers, ate well in the restaurant, won and lost dollars in the gaming saloon – but never forgetting Bob Mason's cautionary advice – and with equanimity accepted that the boat would only go as fast as it did. Like the other passengers, he prayed that they would not collide with any debris which might delay them, or worse still cause a sinking disaster. Tales of boats being struck by huge logs, turned over by swollen rivers after heavy rainfall, and even forced backwards by horrendous currents, were all part of river folklore.

Thankfully, all in all everything went as planned, except that Hal didn't tangle with any young women, firstly for fear that they might somehow be associated with Wyandott whorehouses which he'd had to avoid at all costs, and secondly on account of not being able to put Aiyana to the back of his mind. He felt foolish for his stubborn loyalty to what was no more than a figment of his over-active imagination. Aiyana was a dream in every way, except that she had thrown him off course whether knowingly or not, and he was finding it hard to reconcile those feelings.

Kansas City arrived not a moment too soon. Hal disembarked as fast as he could and left the place without the slightest hesitation. Despite the comfort of a cabin with a luxurious bed, and a restaurant with passably tasty meals, Hal was delighted to be on his own horse, with his own bedroll behind the saddle, a small supply of coffee, cheese and bread, and an open Kansas road in front of him. Life was suddenly very good again, boredom had passed. Hal was now totally focused on finding Jim Crowley. Masonville and Aiyana would be avoided.

Westwards, then south, would bring him eventually to Marriton, the sooner the better.

There is an old adage which says that to travel hopefully is better than to arrive. That was rather how Hal felt when the township of Marriton came into sight after four days of riding. All the time in the saddle, and much of the time out of it, Hal had been wondering how to start his search for Crowley. Although he didn't relish the prospect of seeing the sheriff again it was where he would have to start. He remembered the icy reception he and his pa had been given when they first inquired after Crowley in the Golden Sunflower. They'd been told how he had *gone bad* and then been burnt out and driven away. He was allegedly into cattle rustling. Maybe hitting bad times, Crowley had renewed his interest in the IOU which he had kept all those years and then suddenly decided to call in. It might explain why their herd was taken when no money was forthcoming.

Everything seemed to point towards Norell and Brent being in the pay of Crowley. Probably all five of the rustlers were working for Crowley. If so, he'd lost three of them. In a moment Hal found himself outside the sheriff's office. He dismounted and hitched his horse to the rail.

'Bless my soul!' said Sheriff Skeeter as Hal opened the door and walked into the office. 'Didn't expect to see you back here, son.'

Hal came straight to the point. 'Didn't expect it myself, but I need your help. I was tracking two sidekicks and I really should have been finding out about Jim Crowley. Now I know he used to live near here. Me and my pa saw his burnt-out ranch, and folk in the saloon told us he was a bad lot, so what happened to him?'

Deputy Jesson, who had been sitting quietly on the other side of the room, stood up. 'We heard Jim Crowley went bad after his wife was injured in a shotgun accident. He had a son too, a boy a bit younger 'an you, I guess.'

'It weren't no accident . . .' a voice said from out of sight in the cells. 'Crowley done it himself. It was something his wife said by mistake. Said the boy wasn't Crowley's. Crowley threatened his wife with a shotgun he was cleaning, it went off and she was hit. It weren't no mistake. The boy was standing next to him when it went off, he laid Crowley out with one punch and took off.'

While the prisoner was speaking, Hal walked down the passageway to the cells. 'You're still here!' he said with both surprise and suspicion. He went back into the office. 'What's going on, sheriff, I thought this man was going to stand trial.'

'He is,' Sheriff Skeeter replied. 'The county judge isn't due till next week.'

But Hal's brain was already at work. 'Listen,' he said,

'that lying sonofabitch said he didn't know Jim Crowley when I asked him last time. Same as he said he didn't know me.'

Deputy Jesson went towards the cells. 'That's right,' he said disappearing down the passage. 'You're a lying little runt,' he said to the prisoner. 'Remember what I did to your leg, last time?'

Hal approached the sheriff's desk and raised his hand questioningly. 'Can I ask you a favour?'

'Give it a go.'

'I've a hunch this man knows a lot more than he is telling. He knows Crowley for sure. I want him to take me to Jim Crowley.'

Hal put up for the night at Sal's Saloon. Early the next morning he went to the sheriff's office as arranged, and collected his prisoner. Deputy Jesson had cuffed the man's hands and, despite the fracture, chained his legs. He unlocked the chain to get the man on to a horse and gave Hal the key. The cuffs were loosely chained to the pommel, the reins secured and the leading rope given to Hal.

'Bring him back safe, or shoot him if he tries to escape, he can't run anyway with that fracture. We don't really care what happens to him. He's your responsibility for now.'

With those words, Jesson slapped Hal's horse's flank and the two of them set off, Hal in front with the rope attached to his saddle, leading a disconsolate prisoner secured to the saddle of a livery nag. The early morning sun was throwing long shadows across Main Street, eddies of dust swirled in the wind, and Hal had a song in his heart. This was the first real breakthrough that let him feel it was more like a mission and less like chasing a prairie dog. But Hal was under no illusions, he was well aware the prisoner had agreed to take him to Crowley's ranch simply for the chance of escape.

For a desperate man facing a cattle rustler's noose, anything is better than being cooped up in a cell with only the gallows tree to look forward to. There was no doubt the sheriff and people of Marriton would hang their prisoner after lip service to the due process of law and sentencing by a county judge. Cattle rustlers are hated, and vigilante groups were springing up all over the West to bring them to justice. But now out of the jail, all the prisoner had to do was bide his time and wait for the opportunity, which was bound to present itself sooner or later. While he was reflecting on his good fortune, Hal interrupted his thoughts.

'Since we're going to be together for a few days you might as well tell me your name.'

'Tolly, that's what everyone calls me.'

'Short for what?'

'Nothing, that's what I was christened with. Just Tolly.'

'Well, Tolly, just to make things clear, I want you to know I won't shoot to kill if you try to escape. . . .'

'I didn't think you would,' Tolly said with too much bravado.

'At the slightest hint, you get two shots, one in each knee, and don't think any different. Like my pa, you'll never walk again. This is no game for me, and it won't be for you, either. You'd better take me straight to Crowley's hideout or you'll wish I'd left you to hang in Marriton.'

'It's a ranch, not a hideout. Thousands of acres, but the ranch house is well hidden and there's always guards around the place.'

'And all the beef is stolen.'

'Mebbe.'

'So what do you think Crowley will do with you when he

finds out you've led me to his place?'

'I ain't scared of Crowley. He's nothing to me. I'll deal with him if I have to. Just don't bring me face to face.'

The last remark puzzled Hal and the conversation stopped at that point. In fact there was nothing more to say. Hal was chewing over what he would do when he himself came face to face with Crowley. He felt he had all the evidence he needed to bring the man to trial for cattle rustling, if nothing else. It would be difficult to prove he was responsible for the fire which killed his ma, or get him convicted for leaving his pa paralysed. If it turned out that Crowley was indeed behind it all, then Hal had already made up his mind that he'd kill him.

That first night, Hal made a camp fire and cooked up some beans and pork. He'd made coffee for them both, and when it was time to turn in, drove a large stake into the ground and attached Tolly's leg chain to it, which fixed him firmly in place. He secured a rope round the handcuffs and looped it round a fallen log. There was simply no chance of escape and with that reassuring thought Hal settled himself in his bedroll and wished Tolly a cheery good night. There was no reply.

The snorting of the hobbled horses woke Hal before the sun had brought daylight to all the corners of their campsite. He rekindled the fire and soon had a pot of water ready to boil. He kicked Tolly's bedroll to bring him to life and unhitched him from the stake, leaving him attached to the fallen tree.

'So how many days from here do you reckon?' Hal asked, handing Tolly a mug of coffee.

'Tomorrow might see us in the right place,' was the drowsy reply, as he stretched his arms to bring them back to life. 'Or the next day. I never thought my cell in Marriton was comfortable until just now, lying here cold and stiff, pegged out like a cowhide.'

They were soon on the road again, and the day's ride was long and uninteresting. Conversation was sparse, Hal constantly aware that this young man had been one of the two who'd brought the IOU to the ranch, was involved in the fire, and was part of the gang that rustled the cattle. There was no love lost. Hal looked at Tolly. Hal was just over twenty-two, and his prisoner was perhaps a couple of years younger, three maybe. He was well built in a stocky kind of way, thick set with eyes a touch too close, giving him a mean look. Hal wondered what had happened in his life to turn him into a cattle rustler? *There but for the grace of God*, was one of Hal's pa's favourite sayings, and Hal reflected on how some people do well in life, and others go down the river like so much worthless debris. Well, it wasn't for Hal to fathom God's mysterious ways, he was on a mission, and the sooner it came to a conclusion the better. If Tolly was right, there might be just one more night between Hal and a meeting with Jim Crowley.

CHAPTER 13

Hal was keen to get going. The fire was blazing with renewed vigour long before sun-up. Breakfast was taken quickly without so much as a word of conversation. Hal was focused on just one thing – how he was going to deal with Jim Crowley. If only that was all he had to worry about. He was in danger of overlooking two other key factors: keeping Tolly secure out of the way, and the matter of the guards. It was almost certain that two of them would be Nickel Brent and Bart Harvey. Since Tolly had called them *guards* it was likely they'd be on the lookout for any casual visitors. Riding down the main track was going to be out of the question.

'So how do I get to the ranch house without being seen?' Hal said, following his own train of thought.

'What?'

'The ranch house. If there are guards all over the place, how do I get to the house without being seen?'

'There's no way that's happening,' Tolly replied emphatically.

'There must be an approach that's not covered. How many guards are there?'

'One or two.'

'Is that all?' queried Hal.

Tolly made no reply, and his silence set Hal thinking. He was now starting to distrust Tolly. If this operation that Crowley was leading consisted of at least five rustlers that Hal and the posse from Duport had already come across, then there were going to be more than one or two lookouts at the ranch. He'd already been given false information by Aiyana, carefully planted by Norell and Brent. It seemed Tolly might also have the habit of being frugal with the truth. It was time to take the gloves off. Hal pulled up the horses. He turned to face Tolly.

'Seems like I'm going to have to give you an incentive to co-operate.'

'What d'yer mean?'

'I mean I didn't bring you along for the ride. You heard the sheriff say you were my responsibility – well, you can just as easily fall down a ravine and break your neck, as stay on the horse with me leading it. Do you get my drift?'

'You ain't got no drift, mister, you're not like my kind, you're more greenhorn than bighorn. You ain't got a clue what you're goin' to do. You'll get yourself shot as soon as we get anywhere near. . . .'

'And that's how you're going to get free, isn't it? Rescued by your buddies, that's why you're keen to get me to the ranch, and then try your luck. Yeah, well I've already thought of that one. You're not going anywhere near the ranch house. You're going to be staked out real good where no one can find you, and you'll just have to hope I get back to you alive, or you'll be wishing you'll die quickly before the vultures start pecking at your eyes. Leastways you won't actually see them eating the rest of you. Now what do you say to that?'

Tolly spat on the ground.

'Good,' said Hal, 'I like a man with guts. Vultures do too.' Then he suddenly leant across and delivered a hammer-like punch directly into Tolly's midriff. Tolly cried out in pain and surprise, falling from the saddle and dangling, until with considerable difficulty managing to right himself, stretched beside the horse with the handcuffs still attached to the pommel, gasping for breath. Hal said no more but spurred his horse into a slow trot so Tolly was forced to limp beside his horse. Seeing that he was just about staying upright, Hal broke into a canter and Tolly immediately lost his footing, his boots kicking up dust as he was dragged along. Hal pulled up sharply.

'Oh dear, Tolly, I hadn't noticed that you'd slipped off.' But he did see the blood that was flowing from his wrists where the handcuffs had twisted round and round, chaffing and cutting the skin. He got off and gave his prisoner a leg-up into the saddle. Shocked by the last few minutes, Tolly said nothing and avoided all eye contact while trying to hide the excruciating pain in his fractured leg. His bravado had dissipated, and Hal, taking no pleasure in the violence, felt he had made his point. Thereafter, at each fork and crossroads, Hal had turned to Tolly and without any words Tolly had simply gestured with a nod of the head which direction to follow.

It wasn't only Tolly who was shocked. Hal had surprised himself at the gratuitous violence done to a person who had absolutely no means of self-defence, couldn't ward off blows or even maintain his balance in the saddle. It was reminiscent of dogs baiting a chained bear, but at least the bear had the use of its claws, unlike Tolly's chained hands. Was Hal being dehumanized by this mission, or was it the entirely justifiable response to much-hated cattle rustlers who had been responsible for the death of his ma and the life-changing injuries to his pa? If only he could dismiss it as reasonably as that – but that didn't account for the shooting of the man upstairs in Bob Mason's saloon, or shooting Billie's father in van Dinkel's cabin. Both times in self-defence, out of necessity. But it wasn't hard to see how a single incident to loved ones could turn a man from a law-abiding citizen into judge, jury and summary executioner. The worst of it was that Hal suspected the killing hadn't yet come to an end.

Partly on account of that outburst of unwarranted violence, a sign of growing anxiety and frustration, and partly on account of Hal's feeling of remorse, the progress that day was not what he had hoped. By nightfall they were still some distance from Crowley's ranch. But the sky was clear and the moon was bright, so Hal decided not to stop. He told Tolly they were going to ride until the ranch came into sight so Hal could stake out the lie of the land before dawn, a time when everyone was at their point of least resistance. After another four hours of trekking Hal pulled up.

'Tell me how far now?'

'No more 'an a couple miles.' It was the first time Tolly had spoken since being knocked off his horse.

They moved on until Tolly said, 'There. That gateway's the entrance. For you, hell is at the end of that track.'

'Not for me, Tolly, maybe for you and everyone else down there. Now I've a mind to ride back a short ways and peg you out to dry. It'll be good and hot when the sun comes up.'

But that wasn't Hal's entire strategy. Tolly was going to be a hostage, a human shield, although he didn't yet know it. They rode back the way they had come and turned off the track. Finding a suitably secluded culvert Hal sat Tolly down amongst the willows and roped him to a sturdy trunk. Using

Tolly's own bandana he gagged him to prevent any distress noises from attracting passers-by, although it would be some hours before anyone might come riding that way. The horses were hobbled and Hal left the scene. Skirting well away from the main gate he came to a perimeter fence, no more than a post and double rail, easily crossed, and in the distance lamplight indicated dwellings.

Cautiously, but as quickly as stealth would permit, Hal crossed the intervening pasture, constantly alert for the guards which Tolly had mentioned. But he saw none, and soon came to the edge of the yard. Here there was a conglomeration of buildings – a ranch house, a bunkhouse, sheds, railed enclosures, a large fenced corral, two barns and other low structures such as woodsheds and outhouses. There was no sign of life, and no sign of any animals, just a couple of lanterns spreading a dim glow across the yard. Infiltration had seemed all too easy, worryingly so, almost as if the inhabitants had already left.

Satisfied that he had staked out the extent of the buildings, Hal decided to investigate the barns. Easing open a small door cut into the main barn doors, Hal stepped inside. It was very dark, but his eyes being accustomed, he saw at once that this was an all but abandoned structure without any of the trappings of a building in daily use. The second barn was likewise an eerie shell, with few signs of activity. Something was definitely not right, and Hal's hackles were up. A horse snorted. To the back of this second barn was a separate stabling area, and in it were three horses, saddles and tack hanging on pegs and racks. Three. Hal smiled to himself – Crowley, Norell and Brent. Could that be it? All that talk of guards and lots of men. But why was the place almost deserted?

Retracing his steps Hal regained the culvert by first light.

Tolly was asleep and hadn't heard him coming.

'Well, well,' said Hal, close to the sleeping figure which leapt into life with a start. 'You're a lying sonofabitch. No guards, no lookouts, nothing at all, just three horses. Just like you tried to send me off on a wild turkey chase to St Louis. What do you say to that? You know I was a bit shocked when I knocked you off your horse. It seemed a mean thing to do. But I've a mind to do a lot more until I get some truth. Do you want to co-operate?'

Tolly shook his head and was clearly mouthing insults and dire warnings which would have shocked Hal if it hadn't been for the gag.

'Too bad,' Hal said. 'It's time we made an entrance.'

While he was untying Tolly from the tree he told him that by his reckoning Crowley was indeed the man leading the gang, but the gang was a lot smaller than Tolly would have him believe. Probably just Crowley and the five other rustlers. Two of them already shot to death, and only Norell and Brent were left – besides Tolly, of course, but he was already as good as convicted and hanged anyway. Perhaps Norell and Brent had returned to the ranch and warned that a posse was on their trail. Maybe Crowley had started to move his operation somewhere further away, and they were just on the point of clearing out. Maybe they were still planning another jailbreak at Marriton to get Tolly out, but it didn't look like it. It looked a lot like they had abandoned Tolly to his fate.

'Well, what do you think of that?'

Another outburst of expletives was mouthed into the gag and silently absorbed. But the implication wasn't lost on Tolly.

'We'll see if I'm right,' Hal said, knowing Tolly could do nothing more than fume behind the gag. 'Are you a betting man Tolly? What would you bet on their surprise at seeing us walk right into the ranch house, and what would you bet on us both walking out alive?'

Tolly tossed his head to make clear his thoughts on that.

'No good tossing your head like that. Look, I'll toss a coin instead.' Hal took a small paper wrap out of his saddle-bag. 'Let's say for the eagle I stay alive and if it's the Liberty head, I die.' Hal flipped the coin into the air and let it fall on the ground between them. Tolly peered down, then knelt to be sure. He looked up at Hal and shook his head, a defiant glint in his eye.

'The eagle. I told you,' Hal said, narrowing his eyes. He drew his gun and indicated to Tolly to start walking.

There was still no sign of movement in the yard when they reached the first of the two barns. Hal took a halter rope from a peg and tied Tolly's legs so he could continue to limp but only very slowly. He shoved him onwards into the second barn and down to the three horses at the far end, which he likewise hobbled so that nobody could make a quick getaway. He had only just finished tying the third horse when the barn door opened. A whistling figure entered. Hal quickly pulled Tolly into the shadows and hid as best as he could.

The whistling stopped. 'Hey, what's going on here?' the man said to himself, coming down to the horses and bending to check on one of the hobbles. 'Well, I . . .' was as far as he got before the butt of Hal's revolver sent him crashing to the floor in a spread-eagled heap. Wasting no time, Hal secured the man's hands and legs and tied him to a post. He turned the face towards Tolly. 'Norell, Brent or Crowley?' Tolly shrugged. Hal cocked his revolver and placed it against Tolly's left knee. 'Crowley?' Tolly shook his head. 'Norell?' Tolly shook again. 'So it must be Brent, yes?'

Tolly nodded. 'Good,' said Hal, 'you're getting the idea of how to co-operate. So maybe just two of them now inside the house.' It was more a statement of hope than a question. He smiled at Tolly.

'Well, this is the real test. Now we see if you're up to it.' Hal poked the gun into Tolly's back. 'Let's go and get some breakfast!'

Walking slowly and cautiously, not just because his prisoner was hobbled, Hal went across the yard and up to the ranch house unchallenged.

'One little noise from you and you know what'll happen,' he warned. Then, leaving Tolly at a short distance and crouching low he stepped up on to the veranda and peered through a window. Two men were seated at a large table with three chairs and laid out with three places – plates, cutlery, enamel mugs – and in the middle, a platter of fat pork bacon. A coffee pot was gently steaming on the range. The two men were deep in conversation. Then one of them swung round in his chair and waved his arm. Hal froze, thinking for a moment he'd been seen. But the man wasn't looking in his direction.

With a sudden shock Hal watched a woman come into the room, take the coffee pot off the stove and pour fresh coffee. Who was she? Crowley's wife? Shot dead, surely in the accident. Or is that what he was meant to think? Did Norell have a woman? Or was she just a housekeeper? It didn't matter, she looked unlikely to be a danger, her left arm hung limply by her side, and a woman was a woman and wouldn't be any trouble when guns were drawn. It was going to be easy enough to gain entry with the element of surprise. The two men would obviously be expecting Brent to return to his chair, not a stranger with a hostage. While Hal was puzzling over this unexpected extra person, Tolly decided it was time to warn the occupants. Unseen, he had managed to pick up a stone from the yard and now by swinging himself around he launched the stone at the house. A lucky strike sent it crashing through a window and the two men inside immediately leapt up with their guns drawn.

Shocked into action Hal rapidly took up a position behind Tolly holding his gun to his head and waiting for the door to open, but it didn't. Instead, a face appeared at a window and took in the situation from behind the glass. Hal had to move quickly in case the other man was taking a back exit to catch him by surprise. He pushed Tolly forward up the steps, but he went too slowly and Hal struck him on the side of his head with the barrel of his gun. His prisoner gasped and let out a muffled howl through the gag as blood began to trickle down the side of his face. Hal thrust him forward, then used his boot to kick open the ranch house door.

'We need to talk,' Hal said, shoving his human shield into the room and standing very still and very close behind him, his left hand firmly gripping Tolly's collar, while his right held the revolver, cocked, and in full view of the room where three pairs of eyes and two guns were levelled in his direction.

There was a tense moment of stand-off as all the eyes in the room, which included Hal's and Tolly's, flashed from one to the other to take in the full situation. If messages were being sent they were almost certainly scrambled in the confusion.

'Which of you two is Jim Crowley?'

'I am,' said the man by the window. 'And who are you?'

CHAPTER 14

Hal closed the door behind him with his boot while maintaining close contact with Tolly. His main problem was that while the man who had declared himself to be Crowley was to his left by the window, the other man who was presumably Norell was a distance to his right near the stove. There was no way Hal could cover both of them at the same time, or get two shots off with sufficient accuracy if shooting were to break out. Making matters worse, the woman, petrified but defiant, was not that far from Norell and any shot in that direction might take her out by mistake. One thing Hal had learnt recently was not to cross bridges until he came to them, so for the moment his gun held close to Tolly's head was his best chance of prevailing in the discussion.

'Hal Chesterton's the name. Does that mean anything to you, Jim Crowley?'

There was a short silence while Crowley's mouth chewed over the revelation. 'So you're Chesterton's boy. I heard there was a hothead on our trail, but I hadn't guessed it might be you. It makes sense. Listen, son, I'm real sorry what happened, believe me it wasn't my fault.'

'Yeah?'

'My partner here,' Crowley explained, pointing at

Norell, 'delivered that old IOU as a bit of a joke. One night after a few drinks . . . well, I got it out and showed it to the boys, and one thing kinda led to another. I don't know why I kept it. I never expected to collect. Next thing I knew they'd gone and found your pa's ranch and delivered it. I never asked them to do that.'

'That joke turned out not to be so funny. When they came and burnt down the ranch my ma was killed by that fire, and then when my pa saw what had happened his heart stopped beating and he fell down.'

'Is he dead too?'

Hal tossed his head in the air. 'As good as. He'll be in a wheelchair for the rest of his natural.'

'And Mary is dead?'

'Stone cold.'

Hal watched closely. Crowley's left hand went up to his eyes. Was that a tear he wiped away? He was shaking his head. He looked directly at Hal. 'Son, I never wanted that to happen, you must believe me. Mary was once my sweetheart too . . .'

'I know all about that. Why were you driven out of Marriton?'

It was Norell who answered. 'Local vigilantes. They didn't like what we were doing. They suspected we was rustlin' beeves, thought to make us move on. So we did. They burnt the ranch after we'd gone . . .'

'And it looks like you're getting ready to move out of here.'

'Maybe.'

Crowley intervened. 'I've had enough of this dishonest life, it's brought us nothing but trouble. The last of the illegal beef was sold several weeks ago. We're going to go our own ways, the gang's broken now anyway. Me and Betsy want to move north and start raising our own beef. Make a fresh start on the right side of the law. We'd already got plans, hadn't we Betsy? But then all this blew along. That IOU was bound to lead to trouble.'

'Bad guys about to turn good?' Hal joked. 'I doubt it.' Then he heard the unmistakeable click as Norell pulled back his firing pin. Hal pressed his gun harder into Tolly's temple, so that his head went to one side. 'I wouldn't do that, Norell. I believe there's already been one shooting accident. Leastways that's what I heard. Shot your wife didn't you, Crowley? Was that really an accident?'

'She ain't dead,' he said.

'I heard your son was here when it happened, he laid you out then left in a hurry. Is that so?'

'Something like that. But anyways he's back now.'

'Back?' Hal said, unable to hide the alarm in his voice. Was there someone else just waiting for the right moment, hidden in another room and listening to this conversation, just biding his time, or even now lining up a shot. Hal moved very slightly trying to give himself maximum cover behind Tolly. 'Where is he now?'

Crowley laughed unpleasantly. 'Right there in front of you. That's my boy you've got there.'

Hal almost let go of Tolly's collar, the shock was so sudden. 'What?'

'That ain't your boy,' said Norell, unable to hide his disdain for Crowley. 'You know he ain't your son, that's why you tried to shoot Betsy when she told you Tolly is mine. He always has been, always will be. I had Betsy before you, Crowley. She only married you out of pity, and because she had a child on the way. Why do you think she insisted I stayed at your ranch as your right-hand man. And why do you think she insisted on naming the boy *Tolly*? Tolly is just

142

another form of Bartholomew, and my name's Bart, remember, Bartholomew Norell?'

'Shut yer mouth, Norell.'

'No, you shut yours for once.'

Two shots rang out simultaneously. The deafening blast exploded in the room like dynamite and left ears ringing, the acrid smell of black powder swirling with the gunsmoke. Norell fell to the floor with a mighty crash. Betsy immediately went to his aid, but the spreading red stain on his shirt, the pool of dark red blood on the floor and the lack of any groaning, suggested there was nothing to be done. Crowley was bent double, his hand clapped to his groin and his face contorted in agony, blood oozing between his fingers. Hal let go of Tolly to disarm Crowley: he crossed to the window and took Crowley's gun from his hand, which he gave up without a struggle. But Hal had dropped his guard and carelessly turned his back.

'Put that gun down nice and easy, you sonofabitch, or I'll be forced to shoot you dead.'

Hal turned slowly and saw that the woman had taken up Norell's revolver and was holding it steady with her good arm and aiming it squarely at his chest. He felt she might just have enough rancour to use it. Slowly he raised his hands, still holding his revolver. He could have fired, but there is a line that any man has to cross in order to shoot a woman, and most will hesitate – and Hal was no exception.

'Drop the gun,' Betsy said.

Hal had no choice, he did as she requested and in that moment he realized she was the woman he thought had been shot dead in an accident. It was another of Tolly's deceptions, and this one had served him well. He glanced at Tolly, whose eyes were alight with unbounded glee. His mother had turned the tables and Hal was now at her mercy.

Her first action was to tell Hal to get that gag off her son. Slowly Hal tried to undo the knot which had tightened itself. In one way it was a blessing, standing behind Tolly who was once again a kind of shield, it was giving Hal the opportunity to think how the devil he was going to get out of this turnabout.

Crowley had slid down to the floor, he blurted disjointed words with huge effort. 'Honey . . . Betsy . . . I'm goin' to . . . bleed to death if you don't . . . do something soon. Just shoot this . . . greenhorn and get me to a doctor. I done the same for you, remember? Everything'll work out . . . for us. This is our chance to start over. You, me and Tolly . . . we'll make a new life somewhere . . . I promise.'

'We sure will,' she said with a curled lip. 'I've had enough of your promises. Tolly and me'll do just fine. I'd have gone with Bart and you know it. You gave us the chance when you found that old IOU. We'd already been thinking to move on. We were going to use the ten thousand to start up on our own. Bart, Tolly and me. Now it's all gone bad.'

Crowley's eyes were not focusing. 'What?'

'You're as blind as a bat. I've only ever had eyes for Bart. He was right when he said I'd married you out of pity. Pity because you kept on about losing that girl Mary to your best friend on the toss of a coin. But I made you keep Bart on as a ranch hand and now . . . now look what you've done, you've killed him.'

Crowley's eyelids were flickering open and shut. 'Good riddance,' he managed to spit out.

'And you can bleed to death for all I care.'

At that moment, there was a sudden crash as a door burst open and a man came into the room behind Betsy, his .45 drawn ready to blow anyone to kingdom come.

'Hold it right there, Betsy. Don't make me shoot. You know I will.'

Betsy froze, but maintained her position with the revolver aimed squarely at Hal.

'Jesson?' Hal exclaimed, making sure Tolly was still his shield.

'You're a lucky man, sonny. Sheriff Skeeter told me to track you at a safe distance and make sure you came to no harm. We had a feeling you'd foul up somewhere along the line. Lucky for you I knew things would turn out badly here, but I let you handle it your own way while I listened to the conversation. We've got ourselves a good haul. Kansas cattle ranchers won't be sorry to see the end of this infernal little gang. Ain't that so, Betsy? You and your boys. We've been too lenient with you. Should have put a stop to your raiding a long while ago. When the good citizens of Marriton burnt you out, you should have left Kansas for good, gone right away. Now look at 'em. Only Tolly here still alive, and Brent tied up in the barn. What do you say to that?'

There was a sudden movement. Hal saw it and ducked. The deputy stood his ground. The single blasting shot seemed to shake the room, and the aftermath was played out in slow motion. Tolly fell forwards on his knees, Hal now lay prostrate on the floor, Jesson was spattered with blood as Betsy crumpled like an unstrung puppet on to Norell's body, a horrible hole blown through the back of her head, the barrel of the gun still held in her mouth.

'Oh, sweet Jesus!' Jesson exclaimed, holstering his gun and wiping the blood from his face. He crossed to the sink and splashed himself with water. 'Christ almighty, what a mess!'

*

It was a sorry party that left the ranch. Hal was driving a light cart with Crowley laid out on the boards, blanketed, wrapped and just about alive. Two tarped bodies were strapped across Hal's horse, which was roped to the back of the cart. Tolly and Brent, both securely cuffed, were on horses led by Deputy Jesson. The unavoidable overnight stop on the way back to Marriton was a desultory affair, with no jollity and little by way of diversion. Tolly and Brent spoke a little to each other, but they were laid out together on the other side of the fire. Deputy Jesson and Hal tried to make conversation, but Betsy's ghastly solution at the ranch weighed heavily on everyone.

Jesson gave Hal some more details of the background to the gang. They were not much more than an unwelcome tick on the back leg of a dog. A nuisance to be sure, but not so much as to bring the full force of the law on to their heads. There were no Wanted posters for them, no reward money to attract bounty hunters, but bringing the outfit to an end would be welcomed by the local cattle association. Tolly and Brent would likely hang for their part in the rustling, mercy was rarely shown for such activities, especially when a jury included local cattle owners.

'Everyone's in charge of their own destiny,' Jesson asserted with a chapel-goer's confidence. 'Men choose which path they want to follow. If they take a bad turn, they can retrace to the straight and narrow, or carry on sinking down the spiral. They shouldn't complain when time comes to face the consequences of their actions.'

Making the journey as quickly as possible so as not to spend another night out in the open, they arrived back in Marriton just before dusk on the second day. They stopped first at the undertakers.

Unexpectedly, there were now three bodies. When Hal

146

checked on Crowley he was stone-cold rigid, having succumbed to the loss of blood and passing away in the cart, unnoticed and unmourned. In some ways it was a relief to Hal. He desperately wanted to draw a line under the whole sorry business. Nothing good had come out of any of it. Or maybe there was just one glimmer of light in an otherwise black, bleak and regrettable affair.

When they finally arrived at the sheriff's office in Marriton, Hal was relieved that everything could now be passed to Sheriff Skeeter, the Crowley ranch being well within his jurisdiction. He felt suddenly weary, as at the lifting of an intolerable burden, so weary that after the briefest of accounts given to the sheriff and adequately backed up by Deputy Jesson, he made his way to Sal's Saloon and retired to bed before eight o'clock without a bite to eat. On the next day he would make the journey back to Duport and try to pick up the threads of his life. The thought flicked him back to the burnt-out ranch, the bitter memories and a vision of his pa in the wheelchair. Half-asleep, he sighed, *I can't bring anything back, Pa, but at least what's happened has been avenged and . . .* but before he had finished the sentence he sighed again, turned over, and was virtually asleep before he had stopped moving.

It was near midday when Hal finally emerged from sleep. He yawned, stretched and kicked back the covers. He rolled over to the side of the bed and set his feet on the floor. He sat for a moment, then pushed himself up with both hands and opened the shutters. He opened the window and breathed in mouthfuls of the warm fresh air as it swirled around the top of the façade. He ran his hand round his chin – it was stubbly, just exactly as it had been when Aiyana had done the same thing and told him he needed a shave. He could almost feel the gentleness of her hand.

Grabbing his shirt and hauling on his pants over his longjohns, Hal descended the stairs two at a time and crossed the street to the barber's shop. He hadn't long to wait before his cheeks were covered in a creamy lather and the barber was stropping his razor.

'I guess you must be Mr Hal Chesterton,' said the barber, between long clean strokes of the blade up and down the leather strop hanging near the mirror.

'Must I?' replied Hal, jokingly.

'Yes, sir, you must,' continued the barber, wiping the blade on his apron and lining it up for the first swish. 'There's not much news passes us by. A small town like this one, big enough to be important and small enough to know everyone's business. It's all over the town.' He took hold of the end of Hal's nose and gently tweaked it upwards as he carefully scraped down towards his top lip. 'Yes, sir, the sheriff is mighty pleased. Betsy Crowley's gang is completely finished.'

Hal did his best to hide his surprise without getting cut or a mouthful of froth. 'It was her gang? She was the . . .'

'Best to keep silent, Mr Chesterton, while I go round here or I might take off more than those stubbly whiskers! Why, yes, didn't you know, she was the one always planned everything, according to the sheriff. He said it would have been hard to bring her to justice, didn't have enough evidence. That's why they got burnt out of here. Not enough evidence, just suspicions. Nobody liked 'em. Wanted 'em gone.'

Hal inadvertently shook his head.

'Whoops, that was your fault, sir, I warned you to keep still.' The barber reached for a piece of lint and pressed it on to the small cut from which blood was beginning to trickle.

A moment later his face was wiped clean, and a mirror was held at the back to show the barber had tidied him up all the way round his neck. Hal stood up.

'What do I owe you?'

'Nothing,' was the reply. 'You done us all a favour, Mr Hal Chesterton. Removed a carbuncle from our body corporate, erased an unpleasant sore. Folk are well pleased. The shave is on the house.'

Hal thanked the barber and stepped out into the street. Before leaving town he paid his respects to the sheriff and deputy. Sheriff Skeeter told him to call into the attorney next door before leaving. Hal duly looked in through the window of the attorney's office and saw a man sitting behind a desk. He went in and introduced himself. A few moments and half a dozen signatures later, he came out with a broad smile on his face. Next, he went to the livery to collect his horse. The three horses which had come from the Crowley ranch were his, as rightful bounty, along with everything else from the ranch. He eyed the horses critically and as all three were sound and strong he decided to take them.

Leading three horses would slow him down considerably but there was nothing to hurry back to Duport for. If anything, the future was more uncertain than it had ever been, and dare he think it, bleaker than he would ever have imagined. It was with a heavy heart that he rode down Marriton's Main Street, despite so many men raising their hats and women he had never met wishing him well, smiling and waving. It all felt very undeserved. After all, what had he actually done? Maybe he had been partly responsible for ending the activities of a small gang of rustlers – people with whom he would never have had anything to do, if it hadn't been for the IOU and the gold half eagle. But then, he'd also been responsible for several deaths, and it wasn't his right to take life, that was for the law to decide.

Hal heaved a shuddering sigh. He was keen to see his pa, and get news back to the Holders who would surely be wondering what had become of him. But for all the pleasure awaited in those meetings, his life felt very empty. Such was his state of melancholy, he was conscious of a yawning void which he didn't yet know how to fill.

Not surprisingly, as he settled down in his bedroll that night with the stars blinking at him from the sky, the blackened logs of the fire crackling in the heat, and the gentle snorting of the horses, did he suddenly see the light. What an idiot! Of course he knew what he had to do, especially now he was the new owner of the forfeited Crowley ranch. Once back in Duport, business done, he knew he would be back on the road with a renewed vigour and another urgent mission.

CHAPTER 15

Hal didn't know why he was delaying the inevitable. With each yard of ground on his way to Duport, he was already contemplating riding back along this track, retracing his steps from Duport back to Marriton and from Marriton another four days to Masonville – but definitely not by way of Cutler's Creek! It was unfinished business, he had to know that Aiyana hadn't deliberately misled him, that she hadn't given him the key to the cell just to send him on a wild turkey chase. Was that really why he wanted to go back to Masonville? In Hal's mind, the matter had not been brought to a satisfactory conclusion, he would always be wondering if he had really been duped so easily. But at the same time he knew he was conjuring with peripheral non-sense. He was just fooling himself, inventing feeble reasons for seeing Aiyana again. The fact was, though he barely knew it, Cupid had struck him down.

The more he thought about it, the more he realized that Aiyana had been in his heart, if not his mind, ever since he walked into Bob Mason's saloon and saw her behind the bar. But the outcome of visiting her again had a mighty large degree of uncertainty. His heart might beat at the thought of being in the company of that delightful young woman, but his confidence drained away each time he thought of approaching Bob Mason, hoping to seek his permission to take his daughter away. It seemed like an insurmountable task – he might as well ask for the moon. Perhaps he should toss the coin to influence the outcome. He would be sure to say to himself, if it lands eagle, she'll say yes, and if it lands Liberty her pa will say no. It was with this constant interplay of *will she, won't she* that the miles to Duport passed in a haze.

On the third day, with Duport almost in sight, Aiyana was sent to the back of Hal's mind at the thought of seeing his pa and the Holders. It felt as if he had been away for months on end, so much had happened to him in the meantime. There was some catching up to do, and his heart danced a jig at the thought of being amongst friends again. Proudly leading his three horses he took the track out to the Holders' ranch. It felt like homecoming from a successful hunting trip, albeit tinged with a sadness that this wasn't his home, that his ma wouldn't be there to greet him with one of her delicious apple pies, and his pa might still be without the power of coherent speech. It never for one moment occurred to him that things could have taken a turn for the worse.

A light breeze rippled through the grass, striated cirrus clouds patterned the sky, the familiar odours of grazing beef wafted in the air, and distant voices carried up from the yard. Hal paused at the crest of the hill and looked down on a scene that was more familiar, more comforting than thoughts of a cabin on a steamboat, or a bar in a saloon, a cell in a jail or confrontation with gun-toting strangers. This was the world of cattle ranching, of beef-raising, branding, herding, birthing, breeding, this was the world that Hal knew and loved. This was his country. He gently spurred his horse forwards and went on down the track. In the distance a face was turned up towards him and he saw the figure put a hand over their eyes to try and make out the rider. Hal could see it was Ben and he waved a cheery haloo. The small figure waved back and then ran inside to tell of Hal's arrival.

Suddenly Hal was a young boy again, not able to go fast enough to rush inside and tell his ma and pa he'd shot his first jack rabbit. His ma turned the animal into a pie and Hal was so proud when it was served up for dinner with potatoes and carrots and corn cakes. He'd felt as he was the man of the house providing for his family, and his heart was filled to bursting. But this was no such celebration. This was a sadder affair, tinged with the bitter-sweet memories of what life had once been like.

He pulled up in the yard and dismounted. The Holder family were gradually gathering to welcome him back, yet no one stepped forward off the veranda, or came down the steps to greet him. He smiled at them and they smiled back, but the smile was cautious, fleeting, uncertain. Then he saw the wheelchair, a blanket neatly folded on the seat, and the world stood still.

Mrs Holder came down the steps shaking her head. 'Oh Hal, I'm so sorry. Your pa had another attack, he hung on for a couple of days and then passed peacefully into God's care.'

Hal looked at her as if she was talking in a language he didn't understand. His head was literally spinning, and his brain couldn't quite grasp what was being said. It was as if he knew, but kept blocking the words, his brain wouldn't accept the message.

She tried to comfort Hal, putting her arm on his sleeve. 'He's at peace. He's with your ma again, his beloved Mary.

It's better that way, it's what he would choose.'

Hal had always thought he would be unable to control his emotion, hold back his tears, if ever this should happen. But instead he found himself unable to feel anything, just completely numb.

'Yes,' he said. 'He would never have wanted to stay in a wheelchair. Did he say anything before he went?'

Mrs Holder shook her head. 'No, Hal, he never regained speech, but his eyes told us he knew he was done for. His eyes said goodbye.'

'Well,' said Hal, plainly, turning away. 'Let's get these horses unhitched and out to grass. I don't suppose there's any stew on the stove?'

Mrs Holder smiled broadly. 'You're in luck. I'll just warm it through.'

As she turned and went inside, the other family members dispersed and Ben came down to help Hal with the horses.

'Ben, how would you feel about taking over the ranch here in Duport? Now my folks are gone I need a fresh start. It's something I've been chewing over these last few days and now I see there's nothing more for me here in Duport. I'd like you to have the ranch and the beef. The land already shares a boundary anyway.'

'You know I'd jump at the chance to take in more acres and enlarge our herd with what you and your pa were breeding. Pa keeps saying he wants me to get my own spread, but there's no way I've got enough money to buy anything. What would the terms be, annual rent or what?'

'Would you accept it all as a gift?'

'A gift!'

Hal smiled. 'Listen Ben, I've got legal ownership of a big spread a couple days' ride to the north of Marriton. You'd

154

never believe it, Crowley's wife was running a small gang of rustlers. His wife! Those guys we were tracking, the ones got shot up in Marriton – well, it's a long story. I'll tell you while I'm eating that stew your ma is warming up for me. And look, it's my way of repaying your family for all you've done. A man couldn't have better friends.'

They walked back to the house deep in conversation. Hal ate the stew greedily and with undisguised pleasure. Mrs Holder was a first-rate cook. Then in the afternoon he smartened himself up, cleaned his tack and regaled the Holders for most of the evening with a blow by blow account of his recent exploits. He gratefully accepted the invitation to stay the night and after an early breakfast promised to visit again as soon as the second stage of business was concluded with the attorney in Marriton; and the successful accomplishment of his other mission, the nature of which he refused to divulge. He said if anything went awry, if his plans came to nothing, they'd hear from him by letter, because he'd literally be sailing down the river in a sea of despair, if that made any sense!

There had been a light fall of rain before dawn, barely enough to wet the dust, but the air was sharp and fresh. Laden with necessary provisions for a few days' ride, which Mrs Holder had insisted on packing up for him, Hal left the Holders' ranch with a wave. From the three confiscated horses which he had brought back from Marriton, Hal had chosen a pretty piebald filly which was now attached by a leading rein and being used, somewhat beneath its station in life, as a pack horse. It had snorted its objection, and tossed its head violently, but eventually accepted with equanimity that an unaccustomed task, however lowly, must be endured. Hal had just laughed at the filly's attitude, and then smiled to himself as he thought how well that matched the feistiness of its intended rider.

Several days of solitary riding now stretched out before Hal. There was no short cut that could be relied upon to get him to his destination any quicker, as all divergent pathways would eventually have to cross the largest of the rivers near Cutler's Creek, which was the only place where Hal would have to make his own diversion to the next crossing point upriver. There might be a bounty on his head in the Creek, for shooting the man who'd been sent to rough him up, and he didn't want to take any chances, it was all too recent.

The news in the attorney's office at Marriton was good. Potential buyers had come forward for the Crowley ranch, now that it didn't belong to Betsy Crowley. The proceeds would be substantial. Heartened by this, Hal felt he now might just have the edge to persuade Bob Mason to let his daughter begin a new life.

Recalling again his pa's insistence that *to travel hopefully was better than to arrive*, Hal could see what that odd saying actually meant. If at the end of this journey his plan crumbled away to dust – if Bob Mason refused to part with his daughter, or worse still, if she refused to leave her pa – then indeed to arrive at that point would be the lowest ebb he could imagine. For the moment, while riding his own horse and leading a pretty filly for Aiyana, the imagining of a happy outcome filled him with joy. He felt almost unmanly at the light-heartedness of his spirit. Life was too serious for too much levity, but on the other hand, reflecting on the hardships, danger and disappointments of recent days, life had to be lived to the full and lived hopefully, or there was no point in living at all.

Proud of his amateur philosophy, Hal rode on with eager expectation. He dismissed all thoughts of failure, and in the event of any indecision, he felt sure he could persuade Bob

Mason to let the toss of a coin decide the matter. If the eagle should show then Hal should have Aiyana as his bride, if she was willing, and if the Liberty head were to land face up, then Hal would ride away with a sad adieu. The very next day, Hal arrived nervously in Masonville.

His first stop was the barber's – there was no excuse for showing up unshaven and stubbly. He wanted to enquire after Mason and his saloon, and find out how things were going in the little place proud enough to call itself a township, though barely bigger than a row of façades backed by a handful of residences, yet prosperous enough on passing trade. Perhaps with the proceeds of the Crowley ranch he should offer to build Bob Mason a big new saloon and start to turn Masonville into something of greater note. But then he quickly saw that that might be humiliating and patronizing in a way that he never meant.

He so wanted to make everything turn out right. As a kid he had never believed much in magic. Of course his pa had teased him by making things disappear, or by pretending to detach his thumb from his hand. But those things stopped before he was six because he was always smart enough to figure what was going on. There was no point trying to fool him. But now, he wanted to believe in magic – if only he could make things happen the way he wanted. Before he had finished musing, his face was shaved clean, his cheeks were patted with some sweet-smelling, astringent lotion, and the barber was holding his hand out for the cents. Hal dropped the coins into his hand and walked out into the sunshine. That at least was a good omen.

He was not surprised that Bob Mason in his turn should be equally surprised to see Hal step through the door of his saloon.

'I knew this would happen,' Bob said, nodding his head.

'She has spoken of you often enough. I dreaded the day you would walk back in here. But you know, Hal Chesterton – oh yes, I remember your name – you know, I'm actually rather glad to see you.'

'You are?' Hal said, taking a step back and raising his eyebrows.

'I am. I've got a job for you.'

Hal frowned. 'I didn't exactly come back for a job.'

'I know,' Bob nodded. 'But I've got one nevertheless. And you'll take it for six months.'

'Will I?'

'You will. It's part of the deal.'

Hal laughed. 'Don't tell me, I've got to work for you for six months to prove that I'm a worthy husband for your daughter.'

'That's about it. But you're not working for me. You're working for the town.' Bob pointed a finger in the general direction of the street outside the saloon. 'Across the road.'

'Oh, I get it,' Hal laughed again, tossing his head back. 'I've got to agree to be the sheriff here for six months, to prove that my intentions are honourable. And do I get your permission to marry Aiyana at the end of the six months?'

'If she'll have you,' Bob said, with a broad smile.

'You've got it all worked out.'

'Aiyana has. It was her idea. She wanted you to come back, and knew that you were tough enough to be our lawman. But she's young, and she wants to see if she really likes you enough to be your wife. If you accept those terms, she'll abide by my decision.'

Hal was over the moon, but his feet were still on the ground. Then the door to the kitchen opened and Aiyana walked in to the saloon.

'But Pa . . .'

'Quiet, Aiyana, I know what I'm doing.'

She walked up to Hal and stroked his cheek. Satisfied it was smooth, she planted a delicate kiss on it.

Hal took a step backwards. 'Were you listening at the door?'

'Do you accept?' Bob repeated.

'I might,' he said. 'But I'd like to marry Aiyana first and then stay for the six months. Look,' he said, taking the gold half eagle out of his pocket. 'Let's toss a coin. For the eagle, we marry tomorrow and I'll be the lawman here for six months. And if the Liberty head lands up, I'll even be lawman for a year before we marry.' He was about to toss the coin.

'Wait,' said Bob. 'I've a better idea. The Liberty head is to marry now, and the eagle means you wait for a year.'

Hal hesitated. Bob walked over to him and took the coin from his hand. He looked at it, both sides, with great care.

He looked Hal squarely in the eye. 'You know, for a moment I thought you had a double-sided coin. The two sides didn't feel quite the same sort of risk, the eagle was so much better than Liberty, but maybe I'm just suspicious of gamblers.' He gave the coin to Aiyana. 'It's all right, my dear. No cheating. The Liberty head for marriage tomorrow, the eagle makes you both wait a year. Either way we get a sheriff for at least six months, and either you get married tomorrow or you wait a year. Flip the coin, Aiyana.'

'But Pa . . .'

'Do it.'

Hal's face lost its sparkle despite the tingling astringency of the freshly applied lotion, and the thrill of Aiyana's kiss still burning on his skin. His dejection was poorly hidden. He watched with utter despair as Aiyana balanced the coin on her thumb ready to toss it into the air. The outcome was, of course, inevitable. He wanted to shout out, was desperate to admit his subterfuge, but had to watch as the coin spun up towards the roof.

But before it fell to the ground, Bob's arm was thrust out and the coin was caught on its downward fall. He grasped it tightly in his hand, then passed it back to Hal.

'Put it back in your pocket. You know,' he said, 'I don't trust coins. I say that if you agree to look after the town's law for a year, we could arrange a wedding for next week. Aiyana always said you'd come back for her and made me promise to let you marry her if you ever did. So, what do you say to that, Hal Chesterton?'

Hal laughed with immense relief. 'I'd say you're a very wise man, Bob Mason.'